THE SHOOTING SCRIPT

TRAFFIC

TRAFFIC

SCREENPLAY BY
STEPHEN GAGHAN

INTRODUCTION BY
STEVEN SODERBERGH
AND STEPHEN GAGHAN

A Newmarket Shooting Script® Series Book
NEWMARKET PRESS • NEW YORK

FIRST EDITION

00   01   02   10   9   8   7   6   5   4   3   2   1

ISBN: 1-55704-478-3

Library of Congress Catalog-in-Publication Data is available upon request.

QUANTITY PURCHASES
Companies, professional groups, clubs, and other organizations may qualify for special terms when ordering quantities of
this title. For information, write to Special Sales, Newmarket Press, 18 East 48th Street, New York, NY 10017;
call (212) 832-3575 or (800) 669-3903; FAX (212) 832-3629; or Email mailbox@newmarketpress.com
website www.newmarketpress.com

Manufactured in the United States of America.

OTHER BOOKS IN THE NEWMARKET SHOOTING SCRIPT® SERIES INCLUDE:

Erin Brockovich: The Shooting Script
Snatch: The Shooting Script
Nurse Betty: The Shooting Script
State and Main: The Shooting Script
Gods and Monsters: The Shooting Script
American Beauty: The Shooting Script
Snow Falling on Cedars: The Shooting Script

The Truman Show: The Shooting Script
Man on the Moon: The Shooting Script
The Ice Storm: The Shooting Script
Dead Man Walking: The Shooting Script
The Birdcage: The Shooting Script
The Shawshank Redemption: The Shooting Script
The People vs. Larry Flynt: The Shooting Script

The Age of Innocence: The Shooting Script

OTHER NEWMARKET PICTORIAL MOVIEBOOKS AND NEWMARKET INSIDER FILM BOOKS INCLUDE:

Crouching Tiger, Hidden Dragon: A Portrait of the Ang Lee Film★
Gladiator: The Making of the Ridley Scott Epic Film
Stuart Little: The Art, the Artists and the Story Behind the
    Amazing Movie★
The Jaws Log
Cradle Will Rock: The Movie and the Moment★
Saving Private Ryan: The Men, The Mission, The Movie
Amistad: A Celebration of the Film by Steven Spielberg
The Seven Years in Tibet Screenplay and Story★

Men in Black: The Script and the Story Behind the Film★
The Age of Innocence: A Portrait of the Film★
The Sense and Sensibility Screenplay & Diaries★
Mary Shelley's Frankenstein: The Classic Tale of Terror Reborn
    on Film★
Bram Stoker's Dracula: The Film and the Legend★
Dances with Wolves: The Illustrated Story of the Epic Film★
The Inner Circle: An Inside View of Soviet Life Under Stalin
Neil Simon's Lost in Yonkers: The Illustrated Screenplay of the Film★

★Includes Screenplay

CONTENTS

INTRODUCTION

BY STEVEN SODERBERGH AND STEPHEN GAGHAN

INT. THE DAILY GRILL, CORNER OF 3RD ST. AND LA CIENEGA, LOS ANGELES. NIGHT.

As they did on many occasions while working on the script for **Traffic**, *Steven Soderbergh and Steve Gaghan sit in one of the brown leather booths that line the edges of the restaurant. This time, however, they are looking back instead of forward. It is Sunday, and they have both been working all day (Soderbergh on finishing* **Traffic** *and Gaghan on the new script,* **Abandon**, *he has just finished writing for Ed Zwick). They are tired but in good spirits.*

SG: I wish I could say something interesting. I've been working since early this morning, and I'm completely brain dead.

SS: Me, too. When did you start working with Ed on this?

SG: It was '97. Zwick and I were hooked up by a studio executive. I had come in independently and said that I wanted to write about this, and this executive said he knew a director who was interested in the same subject. But I had been talking about satirizing the military, and Ed said, "I want to do drugs." I thought that was much better, so I went away and we had some conversations, and we worked up some very funny ideas. We went in to pitch it, and I wasn't really a known quantity as a screenwriter at the time, so they were asking all these really good questions, and all I could say was, "It'll be like *Dr. Strangelove.*" And they kept looking to Ed in the corner of the room and he would just nod, like, "He can do it, don't worry." (laughs)

SS: Then what? You started researching?

SG. They authorized a research trip, a really expensive one. I went to Washington and New York. I spent a long time in D.C., using any contacts that Ed or I had. I ended up at the Pentagon, at the Office of National Drug Control Policy, the Council of Police Chiefs, the head of the Council of Mayors, people at think tanks, people advising policy makers about the War on Drugs. And at the same time I was reading a lot of different books, anything I could find that seemed relevant.

SS: Did you have a deadline?

SG: (laughs) I don't know. I'm not sure if a deadline had ever been talked about. I got in that place where I was doing so much research that it was really hard to start. I had so much information. And along the way I decided that I couldn't do a satire, and I really had a crisis. I realized that everyone that I was meeting was so filled with despair, authentic despair, that they weren't really appropriate targets for a satire. They weren't cavalier, they didn't think they had the right answers. Nobody I met said, "We're winning the War on Drugs." I was meeting reasonable people who were having a reasonable response to what they were trying to do. Their goal was always good: "We don't want to see kids throwing their lives away on drugs." I mean, who does? And their response to their job was exactly what anyone's response would be.

SS: They were frustrated.

SG: Frustrated. Overwhelmed. "We're not doing the right thing. What do we try next?" In my meeting with the Deputy Secretary of Defense for Counter-Terrorism and Narcotics, I asked him, "Isn't it common knowledge that sixty percent of the drugs are coming over the Mexican border?" And he snapped and said, "Yeah, well, what do you want me to do? You want me to do nothing and watch it go to seventy percent? Or do you want me to work a hundred hours a week and maybe I can get it down to fifty percent?" I didn't have an answer for that. Everybody felt awful, and it didn't feel the way that *Dr. Strangelove* felt in satirizing the threat of nuclear holocaust, because the threat of nuclear holocaust was an abstraction to most people.

SS: Except for some folks in Japan, who I don't imagine found Dr. Strangelove *very funny.*

SG: Exactly. But with drugs, it wasn't an abstraction. It was the kid next door. Everyone knew someone who had trouble with alcohol or drugs.

SS: But Ed thought you were just blocked.

SG: Ed thought I was just blocked. (thinks) Yes, blocked would be the word.

SS: *When you expressed this idea of not doing a satire, what did Ed say?*

SG: He thought it made sense. Although there is some stuff that is left over from that satirical notion in the script we have.

SS: *The long version of the cocktail party.*

SG: Right. And Eduardo Ruiz getting chased into a children's pizza parlor, those sorts of absurdities, the absurdities of the undertaking. The policy failure. So another seven or eight months went by, and about that time you and Laura (Bickford, producer) came along. How did you get interested in it?

SS: *Through Laura. We were having a career conversation one day, as in, "What have you got going?" and she mentioned she was interested in doing a drug movie and that she had the rights to the "Traffik" miniseries, which I'd seen and liked. So, I said, "Really? Well, I'd like to do that." And she looked at me like, "I hope you're serious, because I don't want to fuck around with someone who's just casual about it." And I said, "Really. I really think there's a movie there." So we began looking for writers and we read your script for* Havoc *(which dealt with teen drug use and gangs at Palisades High School) and thought you'd be perfect for* Traffic *and set up a meeting. And it was a funny meeting because we felt you had all the information and you were absolutely the guy to write this and we had a title and a spine, but—*

SG: I was already doing the exact same movie for Ed Zwick. (laughter) But it was so clear that if we could combine forces rather than having competing projects...

SS: *Well, that's where Ed deserves props for agreeing to splice the two together.*

SG: It was a hard decision for him.

SS: *I'm sure.*

SG: He said he'd gotten to a point where he was interested in trying to produce certain directors that he respected. And he really thought about it and he called up and said, "You know, on this one, I'd be excited to produce." And that's what made it happen. And the thing that excited me most about *Traffic* was the idea of multiple story lines. It had just never occurred to me. It's a big subject and I was being shut down by the massive amounts of information.

SS: *Right. How to get one character exposed to everything you want to talk about.*

SG: I couldn't. So: Great title and a great idea. You mentioned the *Nashville* version of the War on Drugs.

SS: *Right. Obviously, the hardest story was Mexico, which we invented from scratch.*

SG: That was some of the most satisfying work on the whole movie.

SS: *Initially we had Javier as a bad guy, a corrupt cop.*

SG: And I think we could justify showing a corrupt cop and saying this stands for what really goes on in Mexico, the choice you have: take the money or get shot. When we were on our trip to Mexico we heard somebody say that the life expectancy of an honest cop is about thirty days.

SS: *Right. We talked to a guy who was known as being a good cop, and he made it very plain that there was a line, and that if he wanted to survive, literally, he had to know where that line was, because beyond that point, he was in trouble.*

SG: Somebody was just saying to me, "I don't buy the fact that there are these drug lines in downtown areas. If there are people just lined up to buy drugs, why aren't they arrested? I mean, why wouldn't the cops know? They'd know where to go and they'd arrest them!" (laughs)

SS: *They do and then another one springs up.*

SG: Exactly. Or they don't because what's the point? I said, "Well, I can give you seven or eight addresses here in Los Angeles where you can go and look right now." Twenty-four hours a day, you'll find lines just like that. And you might find the police trying to arrest them, but more likely you'll find the cops ignoring the whole system! An ever-shifting battlefield. I feel like we hit pretty close to the bone. And I think it worked in our favor that Catherine Zeta-Jones got pregnant.

SS: *So lucky, because the world knows that she was really pregnant. If you made her pregnant and she wasn't, it would be bogus.*

SG: I first read about it online, and I thought to myself, "Why didn't I think of that? What perfect motivation."

SS: *Yeah. Although, I have to admit, conceptually, the Frankie Flowers assassination was something that we never solved. I kept thinking: we should talk about that. And I never brought it up.*

SG: I remember exactly where I was sitting when I hit that wall. I had all these note cards, I had the outline, and I couldn't figure out how to get rid of him. He was like this dangling participle.

SS: *I think we both agreed subconsciously not to talk about it.*

SG: You know, we were killing three birds with one stone, really.

SS: *And for the life of me if you gave us a month right now to figure it out, I don't know that we would.*

SG: The trick of this movie was what you could leave out and still have the stories be coherent, because there's enough story for three or four movies and they're collapsed into one.

SS: *Right.*

SG: Very early on my job was to determine how much information is the least amount of information an audience would need to fill in the blanks between these things so a given story can stay aloft when it's off screen. I'd never had a job that required that type of discipline. I was going crazy, just compacting, compacting, compacting, and Frankie's death is a real example of that. To explain how and why he's killed in a normal movie, you'd have four scenes. You'd see the hit being set up, you'd see the guy going and trying to get him, failing, trying something else. But in this movie there's simply no room for that footwork. Maybe you hit the moment of the death of Frankie Flowers and you just cut to the director and the screenwriter napping!

SS: *(laughing) Yeah, right. I think we both knew that we couldn't solve it so we just shut up about it. After our last screening, (a major news magazine) complained that there were too many characters and we didn't spend enough time with any of them.*

SG: Well, that is true, but there's this idea that exists in the world called synecdoche and—

SS: *What is it?*

SG: It's the idea that one small thing can stand for much larger things, and I think that when you bite off the idea that you're going to write about something on the scale of The Drug War, you know what? Things have to stand for a lot of things, and one character or one line ends up having to stand for ten things that are kind of like it, but maybe not exactly like it, and maybe in places it does feel like a survey, but you're trying to convey a larger reality off a very specific true detail.

SS: *Right.*

SG: I mean, what happens with this reductionary approach—the idea of needing to know that all cops end up alcoholics or women were left by their daddies—is that you end up with this barrel of backstory cliches.

SS: *I'm just reading this article in* Rolling Stone *about that young kid who shot the teacher in Florida and there's nothing in his history with that teacher or in his life that explains why he chose to go and do that. He doesn't even understand it. But it happened, so you know life isn't just cause and effect.*

SG: And the sum total of living a life is absorbing all this randomness. Shit just happens, and as a moviegoer, I don't want to be subjected to the idea that there's a reason for everything, because it runs counter to my own experience.

SS: *That's why I'm not as bugged by Helena's turn as some people, because I feel even though neither of us would cross that line—*

SG: —we suspect that neither one of us would cross that line—

SS: *—part of the point is the relative ease of it. She doesn't actually have to pull the trigger. It's like: "I can get somebody to go and do this for me." Which is not a huge leap for her, in my opinion.*

SG: It's equivalent to the kids snorting the coke in the den in the suburb of Cincinnati. They're doing something that is fun and feels great and meanwhile, down in Mexico, people are dying to make sure that product can get there.

SS: *Yeah.*

SG: It's that slippery a slope. You don't think about it, but you can pull them out of the headlines and they cross our psyche every day. The kids in the trunk being driven into the lake: "I couldn't keep my kids because I didn't think my young lover would want them." I think there are a lot of people who would make Helena's choice. "All I have to do is make a phone call and this goes away and my life turns normal." How many times does the person next door do something absolutely horrific and everybody just says: I had no idea. I mean, Mrs. Michael

Milken wasn't sitting around going, "Yeah, I knew my husband was sitting on top this pyramid of deceit." It was: He works a hundred hours a week, he flies away in a helicopter in the morning, he goes to this huge office where he does all this important stuff, then he comes back.

SS: Right.

SG: And also, most people smoke some pot on the weekend and have a drink and you know what? They grow old and they have kids, they have jobs, they become grandparents. That's most people. But basically seven percent of the population isn't like that. For seven percent of the population, like my friend who died the night before we started shooting this movie, it's a different system and you can't explain that to Jesse Helms—that it's not a lack of will power. It affects these people *differently.* You can have two people side by side, identical, one person can deal and one person can't, and if you can't, the pursuit of that thing will take you to places that are simply not logical. They'll take you into the inner city where everybody is a different race than you, everybody has antipathy towards you, everybody is armed, and people are engaged in illegal operations with drugs and death around it all the time. You're leaving your comfy, million-dollar house in your upper-middle class suburb and actively seeking danger. That's not what most people do, but that is what some people do and I think that applies to the decision that Helena makes to save her family and I think it applies to the career decision Robert makes at the end of the movie. So (a major news magazine's) comment, you know, is valid for a certain type of film, but not this type of film. (pause) I don't know. I'm the most biased person on earth, I admit it. I don't have a clear-eyed view of the movie, but I know the process that went into getting it done, and it wasn't easy.

SS: Right. And there's no substitute for locking yourself in the room together and just not leaving until you have something. That's where all the big shit happens. When you're in the room stuff starts bouncing around, and you can't do it on the phone, you can't do it through email, it's just different.

SG: You know, it was a great experience all the way across the board. Every time I ever came to you with an idea, your response was always the same: Sure, try it!

SS: Absolutely.

SG: Give me it all! Give me it all! And that led to a hundred and sixty-five page first draft and people saying: This Gaghan is unprofessional! (laughter)

SS: But even with the basic spine it was so hard to figure out what went in and what stayed out. Laura had been clipping things for years and I remember handing you articles with stuff highlighted that I liked…

SG: Six or seven inches of newspaper articles from you and Laura both. They're still in stacks all over my house. Everyday the newspapers would hand us something great. I remember, very late in the process, finding the article about changing cocaine into plastics, and you said, "Do it! That's it, that's the trick!" And it seemed like when we were working there were more and more articles.

SS: That was the other sensation, of this being the time to do this. When the movie was threatening to fall apart I knew in my heart that if it didn't happen now, it wouldn't happen, that a year later I wouldn't feel the same. Maybe because it's an election year, I don't know. It just feels to me like people want to talk about this now, but they don't have a forum or a reason to talk about it, and a movie that addresses it in a certain way could open this gate of discussion. We'll know in a couple of months, I guess. We could be completely wrong. But I think all of us tried to avoid having the film itself be infected with the idea that it's Important. The modus operandi was to be as dispassionate and detailed as we could and to let the rest of it go. To disguise our theme a little.

SG: I heard someone say once, in response to being asked what the theme of their work was: The theme is to not get hit in the head with a shovel.

SS: That's great.

SG: I don't think movies are the place for serious policy debates. All I wanted to do was engender in the moviegoer the feeling of "Jesus, this is really something." Even if they couldn't articulate a point of view, or even if they never came to a point of view, I wanted to give them that sense of: Out there somewhere is a system, an entrenched system that is wrecking peoples lives. Having seen the movie a number of times now, I think it works that way. I don't know. Maybe all of my friends are lying to me.

SS: Jeez, I hope not. I guess we'll see.

At this point their meals were finished long ago and the restaurant employees were waiting for them to leave. They shut off the recorder and each headed home.

TRAFFIC

by

Stephen Gaghan

FADE IN:

1   EXT. COLUMBUS, OHIO - DAY   1

The state capital of Ohio. It's an impressive building for a
city this size.

SUPERTITLE: COLUMBUS, OHIO - STATE CAPITAL

2   INT. OHIO STATE SUPREME COURT - DAY   2

In chambers striving for august, JUSTICES listen to a lawyer,
MR. RODMAN, argue his case before the highest court in Ohio.
Mr. Rodman enjoys the sound of his own voice.

                    MR. RODMAN
          This informant, paid by the police, using
          taxpayer dollars to continue his felony
          drug habit, was the link which allowed
          police to raid a private farm. A working
          farm. A farm where honest Americans make
          their living.

One particular justice, ROBERT WAKEFIELD, younger than the
others, is clearly bemused by this performance.

                    MR. RODMAN (CONT'D)
          The government, in its haste, has
          employed an army of criminals whose
          allegiance to the truth is, at best,
          questionable --

Judge Wakefield interrupts --

                    ROBERT
          Mr. Rodman...it's too bad your client
          didn't show as much sense in choosing
          what he planted as he did in choosing his
          attorney...

A polite chuckle from the justices --

                    ROBERT (cont'd)
          Lately the only variation I'm hearing in
          your argument is the name of the client.
          And you can sit there all day arguing the
          ins and outs of *Illinois v. Gates*, but
          you aren't going to convince me that this
          country has not sanctioned the use of
          anonymous informants.
               (beat)
          Furthermore, there is no sacred
          protection of property rights in the
          United States.
               (MORE)

                                              (CONTINUED)

                         ROBERT (cont'd)
          When you make the decision to have
          marijuana on your farm, whether it's one
          joint or an acre of plants, your property
          can be seized and your property can be
          sold.

                         MR. RODMAN
          I'm sorry the court finds my argument
          repetitious.

                         ROBERT
          Mr. Rodman, may I offer a piece of
          advice? The next time you argue this
          point before this court, regardless of my
          whereabouts, I recommend you have
          something up your sleeve other than your
          arm.

3   INT. ROBERT'S CHAMBERS - DAY   3

The office is marble and dark wood. A young CLERK, black, 29,
enters carrying an oddly-shaped gift. They both look at it.

                         CLERK
          What do you think it is?

                         ROBERT
          Depends who it's from.

                         CLERK
               (reading the card)
          Your friends at Warren, Putnam and
          Hudson.

                         ROBERT
          You can learn a lot about somebody from
          this stuff. Three categories: you like
          me, you hate me, you want something from
          me.
               (re: the elaborate box)
          Definitely third category.

                         CLERK
          What would a law firm want from the new
          drug Czar?

                         ROBERT
          Depends on the state.

                         CLERK
               (checks)
          Arizona.

3   CONTINUED: 3

                              ROBERT
                    Medicinal marijuana initiative.
                         (beat)
                    Or am I being cynical?

They both laugh. Robert reaches up and pulls a bottle of
Scotch from a shelf. He pours a couple of fingers in two
glasses.

                              CLERK
                    Maybe there's a book in it.

The clerk takes one of the glasses.

                              ROBERT
                    Not by me.

They toast and drink.

A4   EXT. COURTHOUSE - DAY   A4

Robert exits, trailed by a small group of reporters. He gets
into a car being driven by two security TYPES.

4   INT. AIRPLANE - DAY   4

Robert sits in a business class window seat.

5   INT. HOTEL ROOM - NIGHT   5

An expensive hotel. Robert Wakefield stands at the window,
looking at the view of our nation's capital.

SUPERTITLE: WASHINGTON D.C.

ON THE TABLE

the remnants of a meal. It was a steak and a small caesar
salad. The wine glass is half-empty.

ANOTHER ANGLE ON ROBERT

in front of the mirror now, trying on a dark, tasteful
jacket.

6   CLOSER   6

On Robert in the same position, only now we are in HIS HOME.
It's daytime, and his wife BARBARA is helping him into this
same jacket. As her hands dust the lint off his shoulders we
MATCH CUT TO:

7   ROBERT   7

in the hotel room, making the same motions. Satisfied, he straightens, then turns to look at himself.

8   OMITTED   8

9   ANGLE ON ROBERT   9

back at the hotel room window now. Reaches to the table and lifts the wine glass.

                                        CUT TO:

10   EXT. DIRT ROAD - DAY   10

This is the middle of nowhere. Scrub cactus and dust and a heartless sun.

SUPERTITLE: MEXICO - TWENTY MILES SOUTHWEST OF TIJUANA.

A broken down-looking Police Sedan is parked on the side of the road. It seems abandoned except there are TWO MEN inside.

11   INT. POLICE SEDAN - DAY   11

Two Mexican men, State Police officers, JAVIER RODRIGUEZ, 30's, and MANUEL "MANOLO" SANCHEZ, 20's, wearing jeans, knock-off Polo shirts, and cowboy boots, wait patiently in the car.

               JAVIER
       I had that dream again.

A long pause.

               MANOLO
       Which one?

Another long pause.

               JAVIER
       Where my mother's suffocating.

They continue to wait until there is the sound of a JET ENGINE. It grows LOUDER as it approaches.

12   EXT. THE POLICE SEDAN - DAY   12

The shadow of a large plane crosses the desert floor. Then, an old DC-3 flies fifty feet above the Police Sedan.

13   INT. POLICE SEDAN - DAY   13

They watch the plane disappear over a small rise in the
desert. They look at each other and wait some more.

14   EXT. MEXICAN DESERT - LATER   14

From the direction of the landing strip, a moving van lumbers
down the road, two TEENAGERS in the cab.

15   INT. POLICE SEDAN - DAY   15

Javi and Manolo watch the moving van approach. Javi reaches
under the seat and picks up a bubble flasher. He rolls down
the window and plants it on the roof. He flips the switch.
Nothing happens. He jiggles the wire and the siren BURPS and
the light flashes. Manolo and Javi step from the car,
smiling.

16   EXT. MEXICAN DESERT - DAY   16

The moving van slows to a stop. Javi approaches. The DRIVER
unhurriedly rolls down the window.

                    DRIVER
          Is there a problem?

                    JAVIER
          No. There's no problem.

The driver hesitates a confused beat then reaches for his
wallet.

                    DRIVER
          Okay. I see. How much do you want?

The driver pulls a wad of bills. Javi shakes his head.

                    DRIVER (cont'd)
          You want more than this?

Javi shakes his head. The driver exchanges a look with his
partner.

                    DRIVER (cont'd)
          You want something else?

Javi smiles. The driver gets out and walks to the back of the
truck. He opens the rear door. There are neatly-stacked
crates marked with a SCORPION logo and "**911**." He reaches into
one of them and pulls out a tightly-sealed package also with
the scorpion stamped on it. He turns to see Javi with his gun
drawn.

                                        (CONTINUED)

Manolo, at the passenger side, has also drawn his gun and is
motioning the partner to move to the back of the truck.

                    JAVIER
              Drop the package. Put your hands behind
              your head. You're under arrest.

The driver hesitates. He starts to comply then looks at Javi
and Manolo.

                    DRIVER
              I don't understand. I think there must be
              some mistake.

                    JAVIER
              No, there's no mistake.

Javi motions to Manolo who cuffs both teenagers. The driver
begins spewing OBSCENITIES under his breath. Javi puts the
driver in the front of the Shadow. Manolo follows in the
moving van.

17   OMITTED   17

18   OMITTED   18

19   EXT. DIRT ROAD - MEXICO - LATER   19

The truck follows the Shadow down a desert road.

Suddenly, from behind, four armored SUV's with tinted windows
appear, closing fast.

The SUV's force both vehicles off the road where they pull to
a stop. A long beat as hot wind blows desert detritus past
the truck.

Finally, the SUV doors open and FEDERAL POLICE OFFICERS
surround them like a SWAT team.

The passenger door of the lead SUV opens and GENERAL ARTURO
SALAZAR, 50's, a squat, powerful presence in a perfectly
pressed uniform gets out and approaches Javi.

                    SALAZAR
                  (to Javier)
              What's your name?

                    JAVIER
              Javier Rodriguez.

> SALAZAR
> Well, Javier Rodriguez, you've done a
> very good job, but we'll take care of it
> from here.

Javier stares into the implacable reflection of his
sunglasses. In the distance, the DC-3 takes off and ROARS
over their heads.

> SALAZAR (cont'd)
> We've been following these Narco-
> trafficantes for some time but had not
> been able to bring them to justice.
>   (to his men)
> Put the prisoners in the car. Impound the
> truck.

The men follow Salazar's orders.

> SALAZAR (cont'd)
>   (to Javi)
> One question. How did you find about
> this?

> JAVIER
> An informant.

> SALAZAR
> What is the name of your informant?

> JAVIER
>   (beat)
> It was an anonymous tip.

Salazar looks at Javi a beat.

> SALAZAR
>   (to his men)
> For a State Police officer, you're very
> well informed. Let's go.

MOMENTS LATER

Javi and Manolo watch the convoy of vehicles drive away.
Javier lights a cigarette.

> MANOLO
> Wasn't that General Salazar?

> JAVIER
> Yeah.

> MANOLO
> What's he doing up here?

> JAVIER
> I don't know. Something.

They start for their car.

20   OMITTED   20

21   OMITTED   21

22   OMITTED   22

23   EXT. DEL MAR SELF-STORAGE - DAY   23

SUPERTITLE: SAN DIEGO

Two men, RAY CASTRO, 30's, proud, ambitious, and MONTEL
GORDON, 40's, suspicious of everyone including himself and
always, always the smartest guy in the room, walk from a
Lincoln Towncar toward a dumpy office. Castro is talking
under his breath --

> CASTRO
> No telltales. Nothing to read. Not
> touching my face. Not even blinking. No
> giveaways.
>   (beat)
> How're you feeling?

> GORDON
>   (keyed up)
> I feel good.

> CASTRO
> No more pissant basin league bullshit for
> us, hunh?

> GORDON
> Nope.

Castro stretches his arms, swings them around.

> CASTRO
> Limbering up, gonna stay loose, keep it
> all together. Take this motherfucker
> down.

They reach the door to the office. Gordon looks at Castro,
then turns the handle.

23   CONTINUED: 23

                         CASTRO (CONT'D)
               Showtime.

24   INT. OFFICE, DEL MAR SELF-STORAGE - DAY   24

It's a cluttered, rundown working office unusual only in the
extent of its ordinariness. A SECRETARY goes about her
business like a somnambulist. CLERKS shuffle and file.

Castro switches into Spanish --

                         CASTRO
                    (in Spanish)
               Good afternoon, ladies, gentlemen. We're
               looking for Eduardo Ruiz. We have a two
               o'clock appointment.

25   INT. OFFICE, DEL MAR SELF-STORAGE - LATER   25

In a back alcove, Castro and Gordon sit across a cheap table
from EDUARDO RUIZ, 40's, an entrepreneur in an expensive suit
and bad hairpiece. They are waiting.

                         RUIZ
               You ever buy a quarter ton? Not many
               people have.

Another "businessman" enters from another door and whispers
in Ruiz's ear, then leaves again.

                         RUIZ (cont'd)
               So, it's worth the wait, right? What can
               I do? Rent a Huey? Have an airlift? It's
               not like you can put it in a condom up
               some mule's asshole, right? How many
               peasants would that take? A line
               stretching from here to Mexico City --

                         GORDON
               Nobody said shit, Eduardo --

One of Ruiz's hands dips under the desk where we see a
handgun is holstered on the underside.

                         RUIZ
               Relax. We're waiting, that's it.

                         CASTRO
               Hey, you want to hear a joke? I got a
               joke. Why do women wear makeup and
               perfume?

25   CONTINUED: 25

                              GORDON
                    Chill out --

                              CASTRO
                    It's a funny fuckin' joke and it's quick.
                    Why do women wear makeup and perfume?

                              RUIZ
                    I don't know.

                              CASTRO
                    'Cause they're ugly and they stink.

          Castro laughs uproariously.

26   INT. DEA SURVEILLANCE SPACE - DAY   26

          ON FUZZY SURVEILLANCE VIDEO: Castro laughing. Ruiz politely
          smiling, one of his hands hidden by the table.

                              GORDON
                    Man, you never been close enough to a
                    woman to know how she smells.

                              DEA AGENT (V.O.)
                    What's his hand doing? Watch his hand.
                    Anybody? I don't like the hand.

27   IN THE OFFICE   27

          The room is filled with crappy surveillance equipment. DEA
          AGENTS, in DEA logo'd outerwear, jiggle a monitor fuzzily
          displaying the view from another hidden camera: Gordon and
          Ruiz around the cheap table.

                              DEA AGENT
                    This is ridiculous this fucking thing.
                         (taps monitor)
                    Look at this shit -- the first television
                    transmission. I had better shit when I
                    was the AV guy at junior high, swear-to-
                    God.

                              ANOTHER DEA AGENT
                    Come on, Castro, pay attention. Watch his
                    damn hands.

          ON THE MONITOR

          Another "businessman" enters the office and whispers in
          Ruiz's ear.

27   CONTINUED: 27

                              RUIZ (ON MONITOR)
                    Soon.

Another AGENT peers out a window through binoculars. HIS POV:
the exterior of the office where Castro, Gordon, and Ruiz
talk.

28   EXT. DEL MAR SELF-STORAGE, SAN DIEGO - DAY   28

A BLUE VAN makes a slow turn into the parking lot.

29   EXT. ROOF - DAY   29

TWO FBI AGENTS, in jackets reading "FBI," hide on an opposing
roof. They look through high-powered binoculars. Binocular
POV: the BLUE VAN turning into the plaza.

                              FBI AGENT #2
                    All right, here we go. The blue van.

His binocular POV detects three unmarked cars discreetly
following the van.

                              FBI AGENT #2 (cont'd)
                    Three unmarked vehicles.
                         (picks up walkie)
                    Three unmarked vehicles accompanying.

The unmarked cars split up and one turns into the parking lot
of a fast-food restaurant. The other circles around the back
of a building.

                              FBI AGENT #2 (CONT'D)
                    It's local. Local or Customs. Oh, man, I
                    don't know. Looks like the cavalry.

                              FBI AGENT
                    This is our show. Ah, man. I don't want
                    to share this one.

30   INT. OFFICE, DEL MAR SELF-STORAGE - CONTINUOUS   30

Through the window Ruiz, Gordon and Castro watch the van
disappear into the bay of a storage unit. A man is pulling
down the door behind it when three unmarked squad cars ROAR
into the lot, surrounding the unit, officers exit the cars
with their guns drawn --

Gordon and Castro stare in disbelief.

Ruiz FIRES the gun under the desk which hits Gordon full in
the chest, knocking him backwards.

                                                            (CONTINUED)

30   CONTINUED: 30

Ruiz's men run into the room pulling guns.

Castro dives and pulls his weapon, firing at Ruiz's men, hitting both of them. Ruiz bolts through another door. Castro pursues, talking into his shirt collar --

                    CASTRO
          Agent down. Repeat, agent down.

Gordon gets slowly to his feet, shaking off the blast to his Kevlar, and runs after them.

31   EXT. DEL MAR SELF-STORAGE - DAY   31

The DEA are shooting at the men inside the storage unit who are shooting back.

From all over the stake-out location, DEA AGENTS emerge firing their weapons. An equal number of FBI AGENTS emerge firing in return. Nobody was aware of the other's presence.

It's CHAOS, a clusterfuck of law-enforcement zeal with three competing sets of good guys shouting through BULL-HORNS, GUNSHOTS and SCREAMING.

Ruiz breaks through the corner of the lot, cutting between two buildings. Castro emerges and chases him.

32   EXT. PARKING LOT - DAY   32

Ruiz runs out the back of the storage company. He cuts between parked cars, heading for The Fun Zone, a kiddie restaurant.

33   INT. THE FUN ZONE - DAY   33

Castro enters The Fun Zone. There's a cardboard cutout of SPASTIC JACK, a beloved comedy figure who looks like a rabbit version of Jar Jar Binks, promoting the "Special Edition" glass: "Collect All Four." There's an enclosure filled with colored plastic balls.

The restaurant is empty except for a CLOWN filling out a time card. The clown stands.

                    CLOWN
          Hey dudes, we're not open yet.

Castro makes a motion for him to be quiet and keeps moving toward the room of colored balls.

Gordon enters the restaurant and follows him. An ANIMATRONIC BAND starts to play a SONG.

                                              (CONTINUED)

33   CONTINUED: 33

Gordon sees a half-hidden foot buried underneath the plastic
balls at the far end of the room. He takes careful aim and
FIRES.

Ruiz SCREAMS and sits up. Castro pounces on him, disarming
him, and roughing him up.

34   EXT. THE FUN ZONE - DAY   34

Castro and Gordon shove Ruiz into the sunlight. They wait
while their eyes adjust.

                        RUIZ
              Take me to the hospital. I'm bleeding to
              death.

Castro shoves him forward.

A35   ACROSS THE PARKING LOT   A35

DEA has opened the back of the van where a quarter-ton of
cocaine is spilling out onto the pavement.

                                                          CUT TO:

35   INT. GUEST HOUSE - AFTERNOON   35

A bong hit is expelled into the air. In the living room of a
comfortable, preppy guest house, private school TEENAGERS
party and hang-out: cigarettes in ashtrays, beer and bong on
the coffee table, loud MUSIC.

SUPERTITLE: CINCINNATI, OHIO

The TV is on with the sound off. The curtains are closed.
The four boys wear school blazers with their ties pulled
askew, the three girls' clothing are also identical. Some sit
on couches, some on the floor. They are stoned.

One intense-looking boy, SETH ABRAHMS, 17, wild curly hair
and the attitude of a young Coleridge, and a girl, CAROLINE
WAKEFIELD, 16, really sixteen which means she looks about 12,
pretty and flirtatiously irreverent, sit at a desk in front
of a Powerbook G-3 playing an on-line trivia game. Seth
speaks rapidly and precisely.

                        SETH
              Father of Greek tragedy? Anyone? Okay,
              Aeschylus it is.
                   (hits keys)
              His trilogy? The Oresteia. I mean this is
              beautiful, can anyone stop the Seth
              Machine?
                        (MORE)

                                                    (CONTINUED)

35   CONTINUED: 35

                          SETH   (cont'd)
                     (hits keys)
               Score. Thank you. Madmax from Omaha we
               own you. And Tragedy is closed out.

Seth leans over and snorts a line of coke from a mirror. He
hands it to Caroline who effortlessly does one.

                          CAROLINE
               Entertainment. The Susan Lucci section or
               Banal Love Songs of the Nineties?

Seth looks at her. He has a crush.

                          SETH
               Banal Love Songs it is.
                     (hits keys)
               Hey, you wanna try something?

She nods. They both take a swig of beer. He takes her hand
pulling her past the stoned people on the couch --

IN THE KITCHEN

Seth takes out a box of baking soda. He tears off a square of
aluminum foil. He takes out a spoon. Caroline watches as he
dumps a small amount of cocaine into the spoon. He adds a
pinch of baking soda. He puts in a few drops of water. Stirs
it around with the heel of a lighter. Then holds the flame
under the spoon.

                          CAROLINE
               What are you doing?

                          SETH
                     (concentrating)
               Just watch.

He watches the substance in the spoon as it swirls and
bubbles, then separates... He pours the most viscous part
onto the aluminum foil, making four separate little puddles.

He quickly dismantles a ballpoint pen, making a straw. He
hands it to Caroline.

                          SETH (cont'd)
               Inhale the smoke and hold it.

                          CAROLINE
               What is this, like freebase?

                          SETH
               Not like. It is.

35   CONTINUED: (2)   35

He lights the flame under the aluminum foil. The puddle
crackles and pops, then starts to smoke --

                    SETH (cont'd)
          Go... Go!

There's a rush of thick grey smoke. Caroline catches most of
it.

                    SETH (cont'd)
          Hold it.

She pulls it in deeper and holds... Suddenly her expression
changes... Her eyes lose their focus, her face slackens, an
almost sexual response. Seth is watching her intensely.

                    SETH (cont'd)
          See... Now, you see.

Caroline slumps back against the counter. Seth moves against
her, kissing her, running his hands over her breasts and
body. She stares over his shoulder, holding it as long as she
can.

Finally she exhales --

                    CAROLINE
          More.

The cloud of grey smoke from her lungs fills the room.

                                              CUT TO:

36   INT. WHITE HOUSE OFFICE - DAY   36

The White House CHIEF OF STAFF meets with Robert Wakefield.
The Chief of Staff has the floor; he always has the floor.
This is a man you do not want to disappoint.

                    CHIEF OF STAFF
          Until you officially take over the office
          of National Drug Control Policy, under no
          circumstances should you speak to the
          press unprotected, without going through
          this office or having someone in the
          room. There are a lot of interests in
          this town and, right now, they're all
          scared of you. The reason they're scared
          of you...technically, you have veto power
          over their budgets. So think about that:
          FBI, CIA, DEA, CUSTOMS, TREASURY, ATF,
          DEFENSE, IRS, Radio Shack and the DMV,
          they're all gonna want to speak to you.
                    (MORE)

                                              (CONTINUED)

36   CONTINUED: 36

                        CHIEF OF STAFF (cont'd)
            And that's the good news... You'll also
            be meeting Senators and Congressman, each
            with a specially prepared question. Their
            question is designed for one thing: to
            make them look smart. If you lecture
            them, they won't think you respect them.
            If you respond with utter humility, they
            will. Remember, this is about your
            respect for them, and the President's
            respect for them. Speaking of which, as
            soon as he gets back from Russia and
            China, we'll get you in there for some
            face-time, let the two of you catch up.
                (beat)
            It'd probably be a good idea for you to
            meet your predecessor. I'll have Jeff
            Sheridan take you over. Also, four weeks
            from today you will give your first
            official press conference. In it you will
            outline the President's strategy for
            winning the war on drugs.
                (beat)
            Okay, anything else?

                        ROBERT
            I'll be sure to let you know.

37   INT. EXECUTIVE BUILDING, WASHINGTON, D.C. - DAY   37

Robert makes his way through a warren of hallways in the
endless corridors of the Old Executive Building alongside
JEFF SHERIDAN, 35, an enthusiastic government employee who
has found his place.

                        SHERIDAN
            I just want to be clear about one thing.
            I used to work for him, but now I work
            for you. I'm not a partisan person, I'm
            an issue person. In the next few weeks,
            if you allow me, we'll get you well-
            versed on an incredible array of issues.
            The most important of which, in my
            opinion, being Mexico. I know everybody
            that you're gonna meet. I know what they
            want and why. It's important that they
            like you. It's not important that they
            like me. That's why I can help protect
            you.

                        ROBERT
            Like you protected Landry?

37   CONTINUED: 37

                              SHERIDAN
                    I see where you're going with that, but
                    if I could just say something, which is
                    basically that a guy like Landry is so
                    autocratic he doesn't know how to let
                    himself be helped; it's a point of pride
                    to take every bullet, no matter who fired
                    it, or whether it was even aimed at him,
                    which personally I think is very self-
                    defeating. Now, don't get me wrong, he's
                    a man of enormous integrity, but there's
                    a political component to this job that
                    the General just didn't have any patience
                    for.

38   INT. OFFICE OF NATIONAL DRUG CONTROL POLICY - DAY   38

Robert and Sheridan enter the office of outgoing Drug Czar,
GENERAL RALPH LANDRY, 60's, buzz-cut, professional soldier
with a sense of humor.

Landry is putting some personal items in a box.

                         GENERAL LANDRY
                    Jeff, you want to excuse us for a minute?

Sheridan nods and leaves.

                      GENERAL LANDRY (cont'd)
                      (bemused, off Sheridan's exit)
                    Functionaries. Nice people, the *Schedule
                    C's*. About twelve graduate degrees
                    apiece, but it seems sometimes all they
                    do is start rumors.

Robert and Landry shake hands.

                              ROBERT
                    You've done a fine job here, Sir. The
                    Office of National Drug Control Policy is
                    in better shape than when you found it.

Landry tries to determine whether Robert believes this. He
looks around the office as if the policy is hiding somewhere.

                         GENERAL LANDRY
                    I'm not sure I made the slightest
                    difference.
                        (wistful)
                    I tried... I really did.

                                                    (CONTINUED)

38   CONTINUED: 38

                              ROBERT
                    There are a lot of encouraging
                    statistics. The work's just started, but
                    I intend to see it through. You've got my
                    word on that.

                              GENERAL LANDRY
                    You're here for two years, three maximum.
                    What'd they promise you? Court
                    appointment? What? District? Appeals?
                         (checks Robert's reaction)
                    Not Supreme... Supreme?

                              ROBERT
                    I've come in to do a tough job and that's
                    what I'm going to focus on.

General Landry SIGHS.

                              GENERAL LANDRY
                    When Kruschev was forced out, he sat down
                    and wrote two letters and handed them to
                    his successor. He said *When you get into
                    a situation you can't get out of, open
                    the first letter and you'll be saved. And
                    when you get into another situation you
                    can't get out of, open the second.* Soon
                    enough this guy found himself in a tight
                    place. So he opened the first letter. It
                    said, *Blame everything on me.* So he
                    blamed the old guy and it worked like a
                    charm.
                         (beat)
                    He got into another situation he couldn't
                    get out of, so he opened the second
                    letter, which read, *Sit down and write
                    two letters.*

They stare at each other a beat. Then Landry smiles.

                                                            CUT TO:

39   EXT. MANOLO'S STREET, MEXICO - DAY   39

A cinderblock house. Kids and dogs in the street. A face we
recognize as Manolo's peers out of a curtain into the street.

40   INT. MANOLO'S KITCHEN - DAY   40

The ceiling is stained, the floor sags. A cheap radio plays.
Manolo is at the door. Javi sits at a dinette table.

40   CONTINUED: 40

He talks to Manolo but watches Manolo's wife, ANNA, 20's, a
nice-looking, ostensibly demure young woman, as she moves
around the kitchen.

                    JAVIER
          Relax. If they were going to kill us they
          would have done it in the desert.

                    MANOLO
          They wouldn't do it in front of all those
          people. They'd send someone later, when
          we're alone.

Manolo tenses, and throws open the window.

                    MANOLO (V.O.) (CONT'D)
               (yelling out the window)
          Away from the car. Now!

MANOLO'S POV out the window as KIDS play in the car, sitting
behind the wheel.

                    JAVIER
          Even if that were true, they're not going
          to come to your house where you're
          waiting for them.

                    ANNA
          He's right. They'll do it when you're
          walking somewhere, make it look like
          street crime.

                    MANOLO
          Shut your fucking mouth. Nobody's talking
          to you.

Anna sets a cup of coffee in front of Javi and stares at him.

AA41 INT. POLICE SEDAN - DAY   AA41

Javi and Manolo cruise through the streets of Tijuana.

                    JAVIER
          If you want her to stay out of it, then
          stop telling her everything. You should
          learn how to keep a secret.

                    MANOLO
          She's nosy. She hears me on the
          telephone.

                    JAVIER
          Anyway, I don't think we'll ever see them
          again. Everything's back to normal.

A41   EXT. TIJUANA STREET - DAY   A41

Tourist hell. A cacophony of street venders, panhandlers, and
vehicular traffic. Javier and Manolo are speaking with a
flustered young American TOURIST COUPLE.

                    TOURIST WOMAN
          You're a police officer. Aren't you going
          to take a report or something? Don't you
          want to know what kind of car it is?

                    TOURIST MAN
          It's a Brown Ford Explorer --

                    TOURIST WOMAN
          It was right here. It's been stolen. I
          want to file a report.

                    MANOLO
          Please. Filing a report will not help you
          find your car.

                    JAVIER
          The police won't find your car.

                    TOURIST WOMAN
          But you're the police.

Javier pulls out a note pad and scribbles a number.

                    JAVIER
          Call this man, he'll find your car for
          you.

                    TOURIST MAN
          I don't get it --

                    TOURIST WOMAN
          How will this guy know who has our car?

                    JAVIER
          The police will tell him.

There's a beat of confusion.

                    TOURIST MAN
          Why will they tell him but they won't
          tell us?

                    TOURIST WOMAN
               (getting it)
          Because we pay him, stupid.
               (to Javier)
               (MORE)

                                           (CONTINUED)

A41   CONTINUED: A41

>   TOURIST WOMAN (cont'd)
>   Right? And he pays the police. And then
>   our car appears.

>   JAVIER
>   Yes. Better than filling out forms,
>   right?

The man reaches in his wallet and offers Javier a twenty.
Javi waves him off.

Javier and Manolo walk back to their squad car when two
SUV's come to a stop in front of them.

Javier and Manolo exchange a look. The doors SLAM and
FOOTSTEPS approach.

>   OFFICER (O.S.)
>   Javier Rodriguez.

>   CUT TO:

41   EXT LA JOLLA GOLF AND TENNIS CLUB - DAY   41

A ladies luncheon in the Nancy Reagan Dining Room overlooking
a putting green. The bejewelled WIVES of successful men
yammer at one another around tables with rich flower
centerpieces.

SUPERTITLE: LA JOLLA, CALIFORNIA, JUST OUTSIDE SAN DIEGO

One wife, HELENA AYALA, 32, ex-model, with a sweetness and
intelligence that almost contradicts her beauty, stares out
the window at a small BOY, 5, using a putter as tall as he
is. Helena is six months pregnant and radiant.

A waiter brings Helena's starter course. Her friends, NAN
DOBBS, early 40's, post Junior League, a little tipsy, STEWIE
and ALEX, same League, watch her --

>   NAN
>   Duck salad?

>   HELENA
>   Mmm.

Nan can't believe it.

>   NAN
>   Helena, you never order duck salad.

>   HELENA
>   Well, that's true. I don't.
>   (re: her belly)
>   I think someone else is asking for it.

>   (CONTINUED)

> NAN
> Well, he's got good taste. Isn't it the
> most wonderful thing you ever tasted? I
> mean ever.

> HELENA
> It's delicious --

> STEWIE
> They're the most marvelous little
> creatures. Canard. They fly, swim, walk.
> And so cute with their babies marching
> along behind.

> NAN
> Looking for a nice sauce ala orange.

Everyone laughs. Helena is by far the youngest in her crowd.

> ALEX
> It's a very fatty bird. All that winter
> insulation. Just like me.

> NAN
> You mean all breast, just like you.

> ALEX
> You're bad --

> NAN
> (singsong)
> Jealous, that's all --

> HELENA
> I've heard... I can't remember where...
> That it's full of that good kind of fat,
> the kind you're supposed to eat --

> STEWIE
> Unsaturated fat --

> TWO WOMEN IN UNISON
> Polyunsaturated.

> HELENA
> And now there's good cholesterol and bad
> cholesterol. Everything they tell you
> completely changes every other week. I
> don't know why they think we should
> listen at all.

41   CONTINUED: (2)   41

                          NAN
              What I know is ducks, as cute as they
              are, were designed by God to be eaten.

     Nan reaches for a taste and the other women lean forward
     also, a sea of inanity swirling around Helena's salad.

42   EXT. COUNTRY CLUB PARKING LOT - DAY   42

     Helena buckles her little boy, DAVID, 5, into the front seat
     of her Mercedes. He won't let go of his putter.

                          HELENA
              I'll put this in the back.

                          DAVID
              No --

                          HELENA
              All the professionals keep them in the
              trunk.

                          DAVID
              Not Tiger Woods.

                          HELENA
              Especially Tiger Woods.
                  (sharing a secret)
              ... Actually, he keeps his on the back
              seat.

     She pulls the putter away from the reluctant boy and sets it
     on the back seat.

43   EXT. HOTEL - DAY   43

     A modern high-rise on the waterfront playground of San Diego.

     Helena passes the hotel in her car.

44   INT. HOTEL ROOM - DAY   44

     A standard room looking out at the water which is dotted with
     sailboats and cruise ships. The bed is covered with hi-tech
     surveillance equipment.

     The equipment salesman, LONNIE, 40's, who makes a fetish of
     gadgetry, explains the finer points of operation to FRANCISCO
     "FRANKIE" FLORES, 30's, sallow, watery-eyed, in expensive
     clothes.

(CONTINUED)

                         LONNIE
          Gates, Myrhvold, Bezos. I sell to all
          those guys. Why? Because the technology
          to intrude has reached the masses. Your
          competitor, your ex-spouse, adversaries,
          stalkers, they're at the local
          electronics store right now, and they're
          gonna be intruding on you not only
          through your telephone, but your fax,
          cell phone, pager, cable TV, Musak,
          windows, walls, air conditioning
          ventilation, modem, and internet
          connection.

He walks over to the bed and the sexy equipment --

                         LONNIE (cont'd)
          Nobody has these babies, no way, not the
          shiznit.

Frederico picks up a piece of equipment.

                         FRANCISCO
          I want to intercept cell phone calls,
          digital and analog. And locate the source
          of the call. I need databasing
          capability, to cross-reference calls and
          numbers.

Lonnie lovingly picks up a laptop computer with a sleek
device attached to it --

                         LONNIE
          Your Cellular Secretary, friend across
          all the digital wireless spread spectrum.
               (beat)
          So, Francisco, what do you do? You a PI?
          Private security?

Francisco looks at Lonnie coldly.

                         FRANCISCO
          Assassin.

                         LONNIE
               (not missing a beat)
          Assassin, okay. Let's get you started in
          surveillance.

                                                    CUT TO:

45   EXT. GEORGETOWN BROWNSTONE - NIGHT   45

The house takes up most of one of the nicest blocks. PEOPLE
enter and party VOICES drift out.

SUPERTITLE: GEORGETOWN, WASHINGTON, D.C.

46   INT. GEORGETOWN BROWNSTONE - NIGHT   46

A power cocktail party in full swing. This is where most of
the business in Washington gets done.

Robert, scotch in hand, listens to a smug PHARMACEUTICAL
LOBBYIST explain the world.

                    PHARMACEUTICAL LOBBYIST
              We in the legal drug business, and I mean
              Merck, Pfizer, the rest of my very
              powerful clients, realize this isn't a
              war with a traditional winner and loser,
              but an organism at war with itself, whose
              weapons of mass destruction happen to be
              intoxicants. And if you want a body count
              look no further than alcohol which racks
              up 80,000 kills a year. Cocaine manages a
              measly 2,000. Same for Heroin. But, the
              big daddy is Big Tobacco which kills
              380,000 each year, which, by the way, is
              more people than have been killed by all
              the illegal drugs in the last century.

                    ROBERT
                 (faking it)
              That's very interesting.

The lobbyist smiles. Robert sips his drink.

47   ANOTHER ANGLE ON ROBERT   47

in another room. Listening to STAN, overweight advocate for
the United States Council of Chambers of Commerce.

                    STAN
              It's time, Robert, to choke some honesty
              out of these rural legislators; get 'em
              to fess up that it's pretty much Prisons
              or Casinos in terms of their choices for
              economic growth.

48   ANOTHER ANGLE ON ROBERT   48

listening to ETHAN, earnest advocate of harm reduction.

(CONTINUED)

48   CONTINUED: 48

                         ETHAN
          What's the difference between Prozac and
          Ecstacy, you ask? One's a mattress and
          the other's a trampoline. Molecules
          don't have morality. Really, think about
          it: some molecule changes the way a
          serotonin re-uptake inhibitor works, it's
          not suddenly a <u>bad</u> molecule; it's just a
          molecule. My theory: America has a real
          fear of short, intense experiences.

Robert turns away --

                         ROBERT
                    (under his breath)
          Like you.

49   ANOTHER ROOM   49

    Robert at the bar getting another scotch. A secretive man,
    TIM, 40's, nerdy, sidles up beside him and whispers furtively
    in his ear.

                         TIM
                    (whispering)
          Chemicals? Some say problem, others say
          solution. Imagine a cloud that when it
          rains prohibits the growth of poppies or
          takes the THC out of marijuana. Imagine a
          pill that eliminates any psychological
          craving, from Dilaudid to Dove Bars. Law
          enforcement hasn't let science sit on the
          sidelines. Addiction is no more relevant
          than polio or the Black Plague.

    Tim slips away into the crowd. Robert moves away from the
    bar.

50   ANOTHER ROOM   50

    An argument is breaking out between an ECONOMIST and an
    UNDERSECRETARY OF DEFENSE with Robert as the audience.

                         ECONOMIST
                    (to the undersecretary)
          You're not battling traffickers or
          dealers, but a market, and the market
          contains a paradox: if you arrest
          traffickers, you raise prices, and you
          also raise profits, which brings more
          traffickers into the business.

                                                      (CONTINUED)

>   UNDERSECRETARY
>   (to the Economist)
>   Back in the real world, we're talking
>   about Mexico and not John Maynard Keynes.
>   We will spend 18 billion dollars this
>   year on this "war," and the question on
>   the table every year is do we certify
>   Mexico as an ally or not?

Another man, RUSH PHILLIPS, a middle-aged powerbroker,
overhears, then joins and Robert is encircled.

>   RUSH PHILLIPS
>   You want to make a difference, hit the
>   users. You don't jeopardize our financial
>   markets by some hypocritical stance on
>   drug consumption. We're snorting it, why
>   penalize Mexico for supplying it?

>   UNDERSECRETARY
>   Mexico, don't talk to me about Mexico --

>   ECONOMIST
>   It's the stick of law enforcement that
>   creates the carrot of huge profits...
>   That's economic truth --

>   RUSH PHILLIPS
>   Addicts don't vote; they don't have PACs;
>   they don't spend soft money, that's
>   political truth --

>   UNDERSECRETARY
>   We're locking them up and consumption is
>   falling --

>   ECONOMIST
>   The price of coke and heroin has dropped
>   and purity has increased. All this law
>   enforcement has achieved is kids can get
>   better stuff, cheaper. In economic terms,
>   you can forget it; this is not a winnable
>   war.

>   RUSH PHILLIPS
>   Christ, you want to decertify somebody,
>   take Pakistan or Columbia. We don't need
>   them for anything.

50   CONTINUED: (2)   50

                    ECONOMIST
          If you manage to seize an inconceivable
          50 percent of all drugs coming into this
          country, you'll still raise the price of
          coke and heroin less than 3 percent which
          won't affect drug use at all.

                    RUSH PHILLIPS
          Why are we calling this a war at all? You
          don't declare war on your own people.
          Addiction is a little worm that gnaws a
          house apart from the inside.

MICHAEL ADLER, about Robert's age, and as successful, but in
a different way, approaches, catching Robert's eye through
the arguing demagogues.

                    UNDERSECRETARY
          We need Mexico for these reasons: number
          one -- Defense; two -- Trade; three --
          Tourism; then, way on down the line,
          comes Drugs. The President knows this.
          Why's he holding everybody's feet to the
          fire?

                    MICHAEL
               (solemn)
          Mr. Wakefield, there's a situation that
          needs your attention right away.

Robert looks at Michael, squints, looks closer, then follows.

                    RUSH PHILLIPS
               (oblivious)
          One in sixteen Americans is of Mexican
          descent. Mexico our third largest trading
          partner...

51   ANGLE ON ROBERT AND MICHAEL   51

on the back porch.

                    ROBERT
          You're looking pretty good for an old
          guy.

                    MICHAEL
          My work keeps me young.

                    ROBERT
          Which part, getting terrorists loose on
          bail or freeing convicted murderers on
          technicalities?

                                              (CONTINUED)

                         MICHAEL
          The worst serial killer in history - who?
          Gacy - right? Killed forty two people.
          Our government killed fifty thousand in
          Vietnam and lied about it every day.

                         ROBERT
          Michael, you represent drug dealers, not
          civil libertarians.

                         MICHAEL
          We kidnapped Noriega out of Panama. Is
          that covered in your Constitution?
          Because it isn't in mine.

                         ROBERT
          Noriega is a criminal.

                         MICHAEL
          Noriega was head of a sovereign nation
          who made the mistake of doing business
          with the U.S. Government. So, no, I don't
          have a problem waking up every day and
          fighting our government, fighting people
          like you, trying to keep this system a
          little bit honest.

                         ROBERT
               (amused)
          Last I read your clients were chopping
          people up with chainsaws and delivering
          illegal narcotics into this country.

                         MICHAEL
          I hope when you were on the bench, Judge
          Wakefield, you didn't handle the
          presumption of innocence in the same
          fashion.

                         ROBERT
          If I ever return to the bench, Counselor
          Adler, I hope I have the pleasure of
          hearing your arguments.

                                                   CUT TO:

52   INT. HOSPITAL EMERGENCY ROOM, SAN DIEGO - DAY   52

Eduardo Ruiz lies in a hospital bed, handcuffed to the
railing. His bandaged foot is held aloft by a sling and a
tube drains the wound. He is tugging on the handcuffs as
Castro and Gordon enter the room.

                                                (CONTINUED)

>   GORDON
> You planning on going somewhere, Eduardo?
> You don't like it here? This is the best
> situation you're going to have for a
> long, long time.

>   RUIZ
> I am a legitimate businessman. Fishing
> boats. Tuna. Check it out. Tax records,
> everything --

>   GORDON
> Listen you motherfucker, you tried to
> kill me with a fucking cannon.

>   RUIZ
> You can't visit me here. I want my
> lawyer.

>   GORDON
> The amount of coke we got on you means
> capital punishment in some states.

>   CASTRO
> Move 'em to Texas, fry 'em up.

>   GORDON
> We got you on tape making the deal. We
> got you bragging about the quality. We
> got you bragging about your business. We
> got you.

A NURSE appears in the doorway. Gordon goes to the door and
shuts it in her face.

>   GORDON (cont'd)
> One chance here, Eduardo. Make us believe
> you got a boss. No boss, it's all on you.

>   RUIZ
> It's a death sentence. I'll never make it
> to the trial.

>   GORDON
> We can protect you.

Ruiz looks at them in disbelief.

>   CASTRO
> Who do you work for?

>   RUIZ
> This is coercion.

                                              (CONTINUED)

52   CONTINUED: (2)   52

                        GORDON
            That's a big word for a fisherman.

                        CASTRO
            Who do you work for?

Gordon and Ruiz stare at each other.

                        RUIZ
            I know another word... Immunity.

                                              CUT TO:

53   EXT. AYALA HOME - LA JOLLA - DAY   53

A starter castle high in the hills near Mount Soledad, an
exclusive neighborhood with views of the ocean. Joggers jog
to the SOUNDS of tennis and Jacuzzis gurgling, and lawn care
equipment operated by Mexicans.

Behind the Ayala gate we see David playing with his golf club
on the lush lawn.

Workers set-up the party under the direction of a
professional party planner.

A BMW 740il with tinted windows pulls into the driveway.

                        DAVID
            Daddy!

The window lowers and we see CARL AYALA, 40's, handsome,
charismatic, second generation American, in expensive,
conservative clothes, covering his cell phone as he greets
his kids.

                        CARL
            Hello. Hello.

He goes back to his phone call, pulling around to the garage.
David goes back to his game.

54   INT. AYALA DINING ROOM - DAY   54

There are MAIDS in the house and a COOK in the kitchen. The
large rooms are filled with fine art.

Helena Ayala sits at the dining room table with plans, bills
and receipts spread before her. Carl enters and paces around
the room, continuing his cell phone conversation.

> CARL
> (into phone)
> I'm sorry, Jonas. I don't care if that is
> the price you have gotten in other
> countries.

Helena watches her husband pace as he talks. He can't help it, but a portion of this call is theatrical, for an audience's benefit, which in this instance happens to be his wife. Helena's expression of annoyance resets itself into love.

> CARL (cont'd)
> This is America, a different country. I
> am Carl, a different man. So you see,
> everything about our situation is
> different and I believe the pricing will
> be different, too.
> (beat, listens)
> You're a reasonable man... So take the
> weekend to think about it.

Carl clicks off the phone, turns to Helena.

> CARL (cont'd)
> Every day with this guy is like starting
> all over again.

Carl winds down and finally becomes present in the room with his wife. He looks at her. She looks back.

> CARL (cont'd)
> Hi.

> HELENA
> Hi.

> CARL
> What's up?

> HELENA
> Just watching you.

> CARL
> I got that. How was your day?

She pushes the topiary away from her. Suddenly, she seems tired. Carl comes over and puts his hand on her pregnant belly.

> CARL (cont'd)
> You all right?

(CONTINUED)

54   CONTINUED: (2)   54

                         HELENA
               I keep feeling like I'm forgetting
               something.

Her husband watches her, then wraps his arms around her.

55   EXT. AYALA HOME - DAY   55

Carl and Helena step out on the front porch of their home and
watch David play with his golf putter.

OUTSIDE THEIR GATE

An unmarked police car rolls up and stops behind the wall.
Another arrives and another and another. OFFICERS in DEA
jackets exit the cars.

There is MURMURING, then SILENCE.

Helena slowly turns to look at her husband. He doesn't look
at her.

                         HELENA
               David, come inside --

Suddenly, POLICE and DEA enter the front yard. Gordon and
Castro enter the yard and move quickly up the drive to Carl.

                         CARL
               What is this? What is going on?

                         GORDON
               Mr. Ayala?

                         CARL
               That's right.

                         GORDON
               You're under arrest for violation of
               Federal Narcotics laws.

Gordon and Castro spin him, cuff him, and without emotion
begin pulling him from his yard. David is trying to get to
his father. In a kind of shock. Helena trails after him.

Castro drags Carl into the street toward the open door of the
cruiser. He pushes him down into the backseat.

                         GORDON (CONT'D)
               We have a warrant to search your home,
               Mrs. Ayala.

                                                    (CONTINUED)

55   CONTINUED: 55

Gordon hits the side of the cruiser and it pulls away. Carl
looks at his wife through the window.

Gordon and Castro head up the driveway toward her house.
Helena is left standing in the street. NEIGHBORS, who have
appeared in front yards and at the ends of driveways, stare
at her with suspicion. David approaches and holds onto her
leg.

                                                  CUT TO:

56   OMITTED   56

A57   INT. SALAZAR'S HEADQUARTERS - ANTEROOM - DAY   A57

Javi and Manolo wait in Salazar's anteroom. A ceiling fan
swirls the air. After a moment the door opens and an AIDE
motions to them. They stand.

                    AIDE
                (to Manolo)
            Not you. You.

Javi goes into the room.

57   INT. SALAZAR'S OFFICE - DAY   57

The office is Spartan and military. Salazar and Javi sit
facing each other. Salazar looks at a piece of paper.

                    SALAZAR
            Javier Rodriguez. Twenty-nine years-old.
            Graduated from Montessori school. Five
            years as a beat cop in TJ. Three years
            with the State Police. Parents died four
            years ago in their apartment from carbon
            monoxide poisoning because they could not
            afford to fix their gas heater. Your
            sister works in a Maquiladora in Juarez,
            making designer blue-jeans. On the police
            force three years, you currently make 316
            dollars a month.

Salazar crumples the piece of paper and tosses it in the
trash.

                    SALAZAR (cont'd)
            That's your past. I want to talk about
            your future. Would you be willing to do
            something for me?

                    JAVIER
            If I can.

                                            (CONTINUED)

57 CONTINUED: 57

                              SALAZAR
                    I'm trying to bust the Tijuana Cartel.

                              JAVIER
                    What is it you want me to do?

                              SALAZAR
                    A small thing. Nothing really.

Javier thinks about this.

                              JAVIER
                    Does this offer include my partner?

                              SALAZAR
                    Only if he can be trusted.

                              JAVIER
                    He'll do what I say.

Salazar slides a folder across the desk. Javier opens it and
sees a black and white surveillance photo of the informant.

                              SALAZAR
                    His name is Francisco Flores. He is a
                    killer and gun smuggler for the Tijuana
                    cartel. I need to speak with him. I need
                    you to find him and bring him to me so
                    that I can speak with him.

A58 INT. POLICE SEDAN - DAY   A58

Manolo faces Javier.

                              MANOLO
                    This is fucking crazy. Instead of killing
                    us, he sends us on a suicide mission. Do
                    you know who Frankie Flowers is? He's a
                    psycho-cokehead-hitman. A faggot. He's
                    killed fucking who knows how many people.
                    You'd need half the force to get close to
                    him. And you can't get their help because
                    he lives in fucking San Diego.

                              JAVIER
                    Then I guess I'm going by myself.

                                                            CUT TO:

58 INT. AIRPLANE - DAY   58

Robert Wakefield sits in business class. He twists the cap
off a mini-bottle of bourbon and pours it over a cup of ice.

                                                         (CONTINUED)

58   CONTINUED: 58

He empties a second bottle into the cup, then swirls it
around on the ice. He takes a sip.

59   INT. AIRPORT GATE - DAY   59

Robert exits with his briefcase and hanging bag, two SECURITY
MEN trailing him. He sees Barbara and Caroline, his wife and
daughter, waiting by the their station wagon. They wave.

60   INT. CAR - DAY   60

On the way home from the airport. Caroline drives carefully
with Barbara in the front seat and Robert in back.

                    ROBERT
          What's it like?
              (thinks)
          Imagine you're being accosted by a swarm
          of beggars in the heart of Calcutta,
          except the beggars are wearing $1500
          suits and they don't say "please" or
          "thank you".

                    CAROLINE
          What about legalizing everything? Has
          anybody talked about that?

                    ROBERT
          Fine -- legalization. Okay, forgetting
          all of our international trade
          agreements, legalize everything today.
          The Government inserts itself into all
          drug transactions. The U.S. becomes a
          giant pharmacy. Our borders are mobbed,
          lines of people from here to Europe
          wanting to smoke, snort and shoot
          themselves into oblivion.

                    BARBARA
              (lightly)
          Like a Grateful Dead Concert.

                    ROBERT
          Drugs begin pouring out of America into
          every other country in the world. Canada
          is completely overwhelmed.

                    CAROLINE
          What if every country legalized at the
          same time?

                    ROBERT
              (smiles)
          Somehow, I don't see that happening.

61   INT. WAKEFIELD DINING ROOM - EVENING   61

From the hallway we see Robert and Barbara and Caroline
having dinner. A family tableau. We hear Barbara talking, the
murmur of the days events.

In the room, Barbara continues her dinner table thoughts.
Robert has a good deal of reading material stacked on the
table.

                    BARBARA
          So you know we put the case before the
          arbitration panel, none of whom had any
          expertise. Superfund is just one of those
          words. People stop paying attention.

                    ROBERT
          That's frustrating.

                    BARBARA
          It's so frustrating.

There is wine on the table and Caroline is allowed a glass.
Her parents watch her take a responsible sip.

                    CAROLINE
               (to Robert)
          Did you meet the President?

                    BARBARA
          Honey, your father knows the President.

                    ROBERT
          As it happens, the President of the
          United States, my new boss, the leader of
          the free world, has me pencilled in for
          some "face time".

                    CAROLINE
          Will we get invited to the White House?

                    ROBERT
          I don't know.

                    CAROLINE
          How long's the job?

                    ROBERT
          It's a presidential appointment so...
          until I quit or get fired.

                    BARBARA
          Czar for life, just like a real czar.

                                        (CONTINUED)

                    CAROLINE
          That makes mom the Czarina. I'm a
          Czarette. Like Anastasia.

Caroline thinks about this.

                    CAROLINE (CONT'D)
          None of my friends can fucking believe my
          dad is the actual Drug Czar.

                    BARBARA
          Caroline --

                    CAROLINE
          Sorry, but I mean, come on.

Robert doesn't know if she's putting him down.

                    CAROLINE (CONT'D)
          It's great, daddy. It's just amazing,
          that's all.

They all look at each other. Caroline sips her wine.

                                        CUT TO:

62   INT. SAN DIEGO JAIL - DAY   62

In the intake area of a busy San Diego precinct, Helena sits
on a bench and regroups. Detectives move past her. Handcuffed
criminals are separated, bagged and tagged.

A beautifully dressed man, ARNIE METZGER, 30's, super-lawyer,
knows everyone from the top of the system to the bottom,
slick but likable, smart and ruthless, too, separates himself
from a DETECTIVE he's gladhanding and approaches Helena.

                    METZGER
          Helena, I'm so sorry --

                    HELENA
          Arnie, thank God.

Metzger sits, giving her a hug.

                    HELENA (cont'd)
          Can you please tell me what on earth is
          going on?

Arnie looks at her as if to say, "do you really not know?"
Then, he speaks quietly with his hand in front of his mouth.

                                        (CONTINUED)

                    METZGER
I understand. You're upset. You want to
know what's going on. That's good.

                    HELENA
Why are you talking like that?

                    METZGER
Listen to me carefully. First of all,
Carl isn't here. DEA's got him and
they'll hang on to him until arraignment,
which will probably be tomorrow. So here
you're wasting your time. Are you with
me?

He checks to see if this is registering.

                  METZGER (cont'd)
Good. From now on I want you to expect
that every word you utter will be tape-
recorded, that the movement of your lips
is being read. Got it?

                    HELENA
Arnie, this is crazy.

He makes eye contact with her.

                    METZGER
Got it?
    (she slowly nods)
Good. Do not discuss anything over the
telephone. Do not talk to the neighbors.
Stay out of your yard.

                    HELENA
What is he being charged with?

                    METZGER
I don't know, but under no circumstances
would I talk about it here. I want you to
go home and relax the best you can.
Continue your life as if nothing has
happened. That is very important.

                    HELENA
Arnie, I feel like Alice stepping through
the looking glass.

                    METZGER
That's a very apt analogy, Helena. Now,
go home and be with your children.

63   EXT. BUILDING PARKING LOT - DAY   63

Helena exits. Her expression is set as she drives. She turns
a corner in the shopping district, passing

JAVIER AND MANOLO

who are walking down the street. Tourists, drunk Marines and
the homeless piss away another day.

We follow them into a bar with blackened windows and a
discrete sign.

64   INT. BAR - DAY   64

This is a place where men come to meet men. And it's already
lively even at this early hour. Javier and Manolo find a seat
and wait.

LATER

Javi is working on his second beer when he seems to recognize
somebody.

ACROSS THE ROOM

Francisco "Frankie" Flowers has entered the bar. Javi watches
him circulate through the room then settle at the bar. Javier
finishes his beer, rises, and takes the empty seat next to
Francisco. Manolo watches.

Very quickly Javi strikes up a conversation. We don't hear
what they're saying but it doesn't matter because Francisco
clearly likes Javi.

Off Francisco's anticipatory smile --

65   OMITTED   65

66   OMITTED   66

67   EXT. MILITARY BASE - MEXICO - DAY   67

The back of a blue van opens and a blindfolded Francisco
falls onto the ground.

Surrounding him are Javi and Salazar, who watch as two of
Salazar's MEN drag Francisco away toward an abandoned mission-
style building.

67   CONTINUED: 67

                          SALAZAR
                  (clearly pleased with Javi)
              I'm curious how you did this with such
              economy.

                          JAVIER
              Everybody has a weakness.

                                                          CUT TO:

68   EXT. SOMEBODY'S PARENTS' MANSION, CINCINNATI - NIGHT   68

        With its old-growth trees and manipulated shrubbery, the
        large house is shrouded in the mystery of well-heeled
        suburbia. It is very late.

69   INT. SOMEBODY'S PARENTS' MANSION - NIGHT   69

        Somebody's parents are out of town and the house feels empty.
        Big empty rooms with expensive furniture nobody sits on.
        Faint MUSIC echoes through the house.

70   INT. KITCHEN - NIGHT   70

        High ceilings of a 1930's kitchen. Vodka bottles and
        cranberry juice and limes are spilled across a counter. ON
        THE RHODES AGAIN by Morcheeba plays from a jam-box on a
        counter.

        Maybe ten TEENAGERS are partying hard in this kitchen. It's
        weird and disassociated, people wandering in and out, playing
        with kitchen utensils, heavily fucked up.

        There are drugs on a mirror on the eat-in table. Caroline and
        Seth and two friends sit around this table. VANESSA, 16,
        almost pretty, is hitting a freebase pipe and holds the hit.
        FUCKED-UP BOWMAN, 17, super-preppy with a wan, Baby Huey
        face, takes a slug of vodka.

        They are jittery, sweaty, tweaked, fucked-up --

                          CAROLINE
              All I'm saying, what I'm saying, is it
              never seems like anybody ever says
              anything that matters to them, like we
              all look at each other and nod with
              responses we've been trained to make, not
              real responses, just social conventions,
              phony, fake smiles, surface bullshit... I
              mean, we're all small and do we have any
              idea what each other are like, really
              like? Do I know what Seth's afraid of, or
              Vanessa, or fucked-up Bowman?

                                                      (CONTINUED)

Everyone looks at Fucked-up Bowman who grinds his jaw
appreciatively --

                    CAROLINE (cont'd)
          ... Probably, but do I ever say this
          stuff, just say, "hey, I'm uncomfortable
          in this crowd, I don't know what the fuck
          I'm doing, either? I know you're afraid
          and it's okay --"

Seth's words come quickly, they're riffing, totally in sync,
totally wired --

                    SETH
          We act like we have all the answers and
          we're totally invincible like our parents
          seem and their parents before them and
          it's fucking bullshit --

Fucked-up Bowman takes another slug of vodka and almost
pukes.

                    FUCKED-UP BOWMAN
          For instance --

                    SETH
          For instance I know you jack-off thinking
          about Caroline even though you're
          supposedly "in love" with Vanessa.
          Whatever the fuck that means?
               (a digression)
          I mean, what is that convention, anyway?
          We're all these random collections of
          self-interest, and then we just decide
          that now we're two people walking along --

Caroline expels a hit of rock cocaine --

                    CAROLINE
          And Vanessa doesn't think she's pretty so
          she does all these weird fucking diets
          which is totally about self-esteem. And
          she's beautiful.
               (beat)
          And that's not even fair. Because listen
          to me. I'm fucking lying right now. This
          is exactly what I'm talking about... I'm
          supposedly talking about you, making some
          big point about you, and it's really
          about me. So I should talk about me, not
          you, not even the universal "you..."
               (takes a beat)
          Okay.
                    (MORE)

                        CAROLINE (cont'd)
          Okay, I'm worried I'm not really smart or
          that I'm not nearly as smart as people
          think I am, or that my parents'
          expectations have been way too high since
          I was five, I mean who knows they're
          going to Harvard when they're five, not
          that I'm blaming them for anything
          because everything's great, and I may not
          even get in, but we all feel this shit
          and we never acknowledge it and if we
          can't acknowledge it to the people we
          care the most about then who will we ever
          say it too and what kind of life will
          that be?

They all look at each other with love. This is an adventure
and they're having a connection --

                        FUCKED-UP BOWMAN
          I jack-off thinking about Seth. Everybody
          I know does.

Bowman does another huge hit of freebase.

                        CAROLINE
                    (disgusted)
          Ach, that's what I'm talking about.
          Sarcasm. Always fucking sarcasm. You're
          afraid and you think if you admit it
          people will think you're weak or won't
          like you --

                        SETH
          We live our lives by these unspoken rules
          that are handed to us.

They all look at each other, vibrating with the moment --

                        VANESSA
          Let's be different --

                        FUCKED-UP BOWMAN
          I can't feel my hands.

Bowman looks around, squinting, confused. He's chalk white.

                        FUCKED-UP BOWMAN (cont'd)
          I'm serious --

Suddenly, he clutches his chest and begins to twitch. Puke
and foam come from his mouth. He seizes and falls from the
chair. Vanessa SCREAMS.

                                                  (CONTINUED)

Seth and Caroline push the table aside to get a better look.
Other people in the kitchen slowly take notice.

                    VANESSA
          He's blue. He isn't breathing --

                    CAROLINE
          Is he breathing?

Bowman's eyes have rolled back in his head.

                    SETH
          What do we do? Okay. Fucked-up Bowman's
          turning blue. Doctor. We need a doctor.

                    VANESSA
          Your dad's a doctor. Call him --

                    SETH
          He's a research doctor. You're dad's a
          doctor, too --

                    VANESSA
          What kind of research?

                    SETH
          Mapping the fucking pig genome. We'll
          call your dad, he's a neurosurgeon --

                    VANESSA
          It's three a.m. I'm not supposed to be
          here. I snuck out --

                    CAROLINE
          Are you kidding... I'm staying with you --

                    SETH
          He's gonna fucking die right here on the
          kitchen floor --

                    ANOTHER KID
          He can't. My parents are in Barbados --

71   OMITTED   71

72   EXT. SUBURBAN HOSPITAL EMERGENCY ENTRANCE - NIGHT   72

The Taurus wagon races up to the emergency room of Suburban
Hospital. The back door opens and Bowman tumbles out onto the
wheelchair ramp under the fluorescent lights.

The car screeches around the circle --

72   CONTINUED: 72

ACROSS THE PARKING LOT

TWO OFFICERS in a police car see the body tumble out of the
car.

The cop car wheels around and cuts off the egress of the
Taurus wagon --

73   INT. FORD TAURUS WAGON - NIGHT   73

Seth is behind the wheel. Caroline and Vanessa are in the
back. They stare out at the cops getting out of the cruiser.

                         SETH
          Nobody has anything on them, right?

                                                  CUT TO:

74   OMITTED   74

75   INT. TORTURE ROOM - BARRACKS - DAY   75

Francisco is strapped naked into a chair. Duct tape covers
his mouth. His face is bruised and swollen. A cruel TORTURER
talks to him calmly while dumping chili powder into a
container of soda water.

                       TORTURER
          We know Tijuana Cartel gunmen killed our
          chief of intelligence, Francisco. We know
          you killed police commanders in Tijuana
          and Mexico City. Why do you resist?

He approaches Francisco and begins shaking up the soda water.
He rips the tape off his mouth.

                       FRANCISCO
          My father is rich. He'll pay you.

                       TORTURER
          Not the correct answer, my friend.

The torturer puts another strip of duct tape across
Francisco's mouth.

                   TORTURER (cont'd)
          We know that you went after the neighbor
          of General Salazar, a simple alfalfa
          farmer. His grand-daughter was shot. This
          is stupid behavior, Francisco.

                                              (CONTINUED)

75   CONTINUED: 75

Francisco starts to squirm and whimper. The torturer closes
one of Francisco's nostrils and sprays the pepper-laced water
into the other nostril.

It's like a bomb went off in Francisco's brain. He SCREAMS
and passes out. Blood and mucous oozes out of his nose.

76   INT. BARRACKS - MEXICAN MILITARY BASE - DAY   76

Javier stands guard outside a door, listening to the
strangulated SCREAMS of Francisco. He's sickened.

ACROSS THE COURTYARD

Manolo ignores Francisco's CRIES, while shooting the shit
with several of Salazar's MEN, who laugh appreciatively at
something he's said.

                                                   CUT TO:

77   EXT. AYALA HOME, SAN DIEGO - NIGHT   77

Valet parkers in uniforms work the driveway. The party is
ablaze and there are lights in the trees. A Lester Lanin-like
band plays a STANDARD that drifts across the grounds.

78   EXT. AYALA HOME - NIGHT   78

A conservative monied crowd mingles. Helena is talking with a
GROUP of rich people who include her friends, Nan, Stewie and
Alex, from the country-club, and their HUSBANDS.

                    STEWIE
          This is fabulous, Helena. What a turnout.

                    HELENA
          Thank you so much, but I had a lot of
          help.

Helena circles away. As Helena leaves, the women speak their
minds --

                    NAN
          It's a turnout because it's a spectacle.
          Can you imagine?

                    ALEX
          I've met her husband, as nice as they
          come.

                                                   (CONTINUED)

78   CONTINUED: 78

                         STEWIE
              It teaches me a valuable lesson...
                   (re: the nice house)
              Apparently crime pays.

                         NAN
              Silly, you knew that already.

ON THE STAGE

The band stops playing and steps aside as a man in a tuxedo
takes the microphone. Behind the band is a huge "A.L.A. -
Adult Literacy Advocates" Banner.

                         TUXEDO
              Hello. Thank you. Thank you all. I have
              the results of the silent auction...

                                                    CUT TO:

79   INT. JUVENILE DETENTION, CINCINNATI - HOLDING CELL - MORNING 79

Caroline Wakefield lies on a bench in a grey-walled holding
cell. She wears paper slippers and her belt has been removed.
Even youth can't disguise her hangover.

80   INT. SOCIAL WORKER OFFICE - MORNING   80

Caroline is perched on the edge of her chair. Across the desk
from her is a tired SOCIAL WORKER, 40's, who has been
assigned Caroline's case and is giving her the "exit"
interview.

                         SOCIAL WORKER
              ... How old are you?

                         CAROLINE
              Sixteen.

                         SOCIAL WORKER
              Live with your parents?

                         CAROLINE
              Yes.

                         SOCIAL WORKER
              Parents still together?

                         CAROLINE
              Yes.

                         SOCIAL WORKER
              Do you work?

                                                    (CONTINUED)

> CAROLINE
> I volunteer. I read to blind people. One
> day a week for two hours.

> SOCIAL WORKER
> In school?

> CAROLINE
> Cincinnati Country Day.

The Social worker looks up from her questionnaire and sees
Caroline for the first time.

> SOCIAL WORKER
> Private?

> CAROLINE
> Yeah.

> SOCIAL WORKER
> How are your grades?

> CAROLINE
> I'm third in my class.

> SOCIAL WORKER
> What's that mean?

> CAROLINE
> I get A's. All A's.

> SOCIAL WORKER
> You do? What else you do?

> CAROLINE
> (her college resume)
> I'm a National Merit Finalist. I'm on the
> Hi-Q team and the Math team. I'm in the
> Spanish Club. I'm a Thespian. I'm Vice-
> President of my class. I'm on the
> volleyball team.

The social worker pushes the forms she's filling out away
and looks again at Caroline --

> SOCIAL WORKER
> You wanna tell me what you're doing here,
> Caroline?

81   INT. JUVENILE DETENTION - MORNING   81

A cold institutional lobby with hard plastic chairs and bad
lighting. Government workers move behind thick glass windows
with tiny mesh screens cut into them for talking.

Barbara Wakefield sits on one of the uncomfortable chairs.
She's alone and has been crying. There's the sound of heavily
locked doors OPENING and Caroline appears.

Barbara stands and wraps Caroline in her arms.

                    BARBARA
          Oh, honey. Are you all right?

Caroline begins to cry into her mother's chest.

82   EXT. JUVI JAIL - MORNING   82

It's an early morning as Barbara Wakefield escorts her
daughter from the bland government building.

                    CAROLINE
          Did you tell Dad?

                    BARBARA
          Not yet.

                    CAROLINE
          Are you going to?

                    BARBARA
          I don't know.

                    CAROLINE
          Is this bad for him?

                    BARBARA
          What do you think?

The streets are deserted. Their Saab wagon sits forlornly
under grey skies in an uncovered public parking lot.

CUT TO:

83   INT. DAVID'S ROOM - NIGHT   83

Helena slips into David's room and quietly watches him sleep.

84   INT. STUDY - LATER   84

Still wearing her evening gown, Helena collapses into a
chair, exhausted. A TAP at the door startles her.

                                            (CONTINUED)

84   CONTINUED: 84

It's Arnie Metzger, who goes to the bar and pours himself a
strong one. They sit opposite each other and neither speaks
for a while.

                    HELENA
               (quietly)
          I am on the board of my son's school. I
          had a fundraiser for A.L.V. in my front
          yard. I have a right to know ·if my
          husband is a legitimate businessman.

                    METZGER
          Of course he is. I've known him for
          twenty years and he doesn't jaywalk...

Helena is relieved, but she's not looking at Arnie and when
she does she sees him shaking his head in a very definitive,
"No."

Arnie stands and continues talking as he walks to the windows
and shuts the blinds one by one.

                    METZGER (cont'd)
          ... Carl is a very important member of
          this community and when we're through
          suing the police and the district
          attorney and the DEA, they'll have to
          rename the public parks for your husband.

The blinds are closed. Arnie crosses to Helena and talks very
softly in her ear. She's a beautiful woman and Arnie manages
to make this act seem both practical and inappropriate.

                    METZGER (cont'd)
               (whispering)
          Your husband is very good at his job...

Helena leans back and looks at Arnie. He whispers more --

                    METZGER (cont'd)
          Which is smuggling illegal drugs into
          this country.

85   EXT. AYALA HOME - NIGHT   85

Workers break down the party under the watchful eye of the
party planner. The neighborhood is quiet. There is a
telephone repair van parked up the street.

86   INT. VAN - NIGHT   86

Castro and Gordon have visual and audio equipment trained on
the Ayala home. They both wear headsets.

                                                    (CONTINUED)

86   CONTINUED: 86

GORDON'S POV: the blinds covering Helena's study glowing
peacefully.

                    CASTRO
          They're whispering. I can't hear them,
          but I know it. I smell conspiracy. I feel
          the lie vibrating out of the home.

                    GORDON
          She ain't in on it.

                    CASTRO
          I have dreams about this, actual dreams
          about busting the top people, the rich
          people, the white people.

                    GORDON
          I'm telling you, she doesn't know shit.

                    CASTRO
          She knows Arnie Metzger.

                    GORDON
          So does half of San Diego.

                    CASTRO
          You want to make a wager on this?

A87   INT. STUDY - NIGHT   A87

The music is still playing. Helena looks numb. She motions
Arnie to her. He leans in.

                    HELENA
          If all our assets are frozen and our
          "sales force" has scattered... How am I
          supposed to survive? I'm giving birth in
          three months. How do I get through this?

                    ARNIE
          You're gonna get through it, but the
          first thing we do is get Michael Adler to
          represent Carl. We get Adler and we beat
          this thing.

                    HELENA
          How do I pay him?

                    ARNIE
          I suspect he'll accept his payment in
          publicity.

                                              CUT TO:

87   EXT. WAKEFIELD HOUSE - NIGHT   87

A large, well-maintained Colonial on Mockingbird Valley Road,
an upper-middle class neighborhood in the wealthy East End of
Cincinnati. Leaves fall on the Saab wagon in the driveway.

88   INT. ROBERT'S STUDY - NIGHT   88

Robert is looking at Caroline and he's not happy. Barbara is
there, at a neutral distance from both of them.

                    ROBERT
          Caroline? How well did you know this boy
          who overdosed?

She looks up beseechingly.

                    CAROLINE
          He didn't hang around us. He's like one
          of those hippie kids. I'm not part of
          that group. It was a party in all these
          rooms. His girlfriend who I barely know
          was completely hysterical... He's blue,
          he's puking... We didn't want to get in
          trouble, but what were we supposed to do?
               (beat)
          I mean, what would you have done if you
          had been us?

                    BARBARA
          How well do you know this boy, Seth, who
          was driving? You know the police have
          charged him with a DUI and possession of
          marijuana.

                    CAROLINE
          He's a friend. He's also like the only
          one who was dealing with the situation.
          He'd definitely had a few beers, but it's
          not like he wanted to drive. We didn't
          know what else to do.
               (beat)
          It wasn't *my* pot.

She searches her parents' faces. It has been a convincing
performance and she expects victory.

                    ROBERT
          Okay, honey. We understand. You're mother
          and I have to talk.

Caroline is confused by this reaction.

                                              (CONTINUED)

                              BARBARA
             Honey, we'd like to talk alone.

Caroline stands abruptly --

                              CAROLINE
             Like always.

Caroline leaves the study and shuts the door harder than
necessary.

Robert and Barbara look at each other, raising their eyebrows
and breathing deeply --

                              ROBERT
             I think she's lying.

                              BARBARA
             Me, too.

                              ROBERT
             (reaching a decision)
             We'll ground her, clip her wings a bit.
             School and scheduled activities and
             that's it until further notice. This has
             to be handled delicately. Dan Kelly, in
             the District Attorney's office, will
             probably help us out, quietly. Christ,
             this could be embarrassing.

                              BARBARA
             Honey, this is difficult, but we've all
             had our moments. I tried --

                              ROBERT
             Stop. You experimented in college. I
             don't want to hear about that.

                              BARBARA
             Should we take the quotes off *experiment*
             and call it what it is?

                              ROBERT
             This is different.

                              BARBARA
             Why?

                              ROBERT
             To begin with, she's only sixteen years-
             old.

88   CONTINUED: (2)   88

                              BARBARA
                    I think she has to find out for herself,
                    on her own. We have to allow her space --

                              ROBERT
                    Space for what? To O.D. like that other
                    kid? I will not send the message that
                    this type of behavior is okay with her
                    parents. Because it isn't. Correct?

                              BARBARA
                    We don't want to push her away. These are
                    growing experiences.

        Robert looks at his wife, then it dawns on him .

                              ROBERT
                    How long have you known about this?

        No response.

                              ROBERT (CONT'D)
                         (yelling)
                    How long have you known?

                              BARBARA
                    Six months. I found some marijuana,
                    that's all. And a little pipe about two
                    inches long. I talked with her. She said
                    her friends smoked pot and drank --

                              ROBERT
                    Explain to me how you could think that I
                    shouldn't know about this. Explain to me
                    how this wouldn't be relevant to me. As a
                    parent.

                              BARBARA
                    She asked me not to.

        He leaves the room.

89   INT. UPSTAIRS HALLWAY - NIGHT   89

        Robert is in the hallway, at Caroline's door. He opens it and
        we get BLASTED WITH MUSIC.

        Caroline is sitting in a rocking chair with headphones on.
        She faces the window and moves back and forth, back and
        forth.

        Robert calls her name, but the SOUNDTRACK is drowning him
        out.

                                                          (CONTINUED)

He calls again, this time apparently loud enough for her to
hear. She takes the headphones off - the MUSIC stops - and
turns to look at him. Or rather, she looks right through him,
as though he didn't exist. Robert is so taken aback by the
coldness of her gaze that he doesn't speak.

She turns away from him and puts the headphones back on.

                                                        CUT TO:

90   EXT. MILITARY BASE - MEXICO - DAY   90

Javier and Salazar walk across the base. Salazar is feeling
ebullient and it shows.

                    SALAZAR
          You watch and learn. I earn his trust.
          Then more pain. Then I appear with
          kindness. Within a week he will follow me
          around like a dog.

                    JAVIER
          But will he be house-trained?

                    SALAZAR
          When he loves me like a father, he will
          never tell anyone he was here. He will
          freely give the names of his superiors.
          Then we get them and they too will give
          us names. And eventually somebody will
          get us to Juan Obregon and the cartel
          will fall.

They enter the barracks.

91   INT. CELL - MEXICAN MILITARY BASE - DAY   91

It's pitch black in the cell. There's a human in here, but we
can't see him.

Suddenly the door is thrown open and light floods in,
illuminating a very broken Francisco Flores.

The figure of Commander Salazar fills the doorway.

                    SALAZAR
          This is shameful. A disgrace. Francisco
          Flores --

Francisco cowers in the corners --

                    SALAZAR (cont'd)
          It's all right, son. It's all right.
          Salazar is here.
                      (MORE)

                                                        (CONTINUED)

91   CONTINUED: 91

                    SALAZAR (cont'd)
          You're among gentlemen, now. This
          shameful treatment will stop immediately.
                    (calling out)
          Guard!

A GUARD appears in the doorway. Francisco is spooked.

                    SALAZAR (cont'd)
          I want to know who is responsible for
          this treatment.

                    GUARD
          Yes, sir!

                    SALAZAR
          We aren't barbarians.

                    GUARD
          Yes, sir!

                    SALAZAR
          Bring this man a change of good clothes.
          Has he eaten?

                    GUARD
          I don't know, sir.

                    SALAZAR
                    (to Francisco)
          You will dine with me from now on.

Francisco moves closer to Salazar already feeling safe in his
presence.

                                              CUT TO:

92   INT. COURTHOUSE, SAN DIEGO - DAY   92

A packed courthouse. Carl is at the defense table. He doesn't
look at Helena who sits in the gallery next to Arnie Metzger.

The PROSECUTOR is finishing his argument --

                    PROSECUTOR
          This is a man who heads a large criminal
          organization with international contacts
          we can only begin to understand. Our case
          against him is very strong. He is not a
          flight risk. His flight is assured. The
          people ask that your honor denies bail.

The prosecutor sits. Carl's defense lawyer, MICHAEL ADLER,
from the Georgetown party, stands and speaks.

                                              (CONTINUED)

92   CONTINUED: 92

                              ADLER
               My client is no more a flight risk than
               your Honor or the able prosecutor. He is
               a pillar of his community, a family man
               with a wife and child in La Jolla, the
               community where he has made his home for
               over twenty years. As our defense will
               quickly show, my client is guilty of
               nothing more than being a handy target
               for an admitted criminal. Therefore we
               ask that you release Carl Ayala on his
               own recognizance.

Adler sits. The JUDGE makes a quick decision.

                              JUDGE
               I'm gonna deny bail.

The judge SLAMS his gavel. The crowd is on its feet. Carl
tries to get a glimpse of Helena. They make eye contact.
Reporters from the press gallery are yelling for Helena.
Arnie ushers her away.

93   EXT. COURTHOUSE - DAY   93

Adler, Arnie, and Helena push through a crowd toward her car.
There are several reporters there who ask questions --

                              REPORTER
               Mrs. Ayala, were you aware your husband
               is the largest cocaine smuggler in
               America?

                              ADLER
               Alleged, people, alleged.

Helena gets into her car and slams the door. Adler faces the
reporters.

                              REPORTER #2
               Mrs. Ayala is it true your husband has
               ordered a hit on Eduardo Ruiz?

Adler is in a role he relishes. Helena drives away. We move
up to Gordon, who is watching from the hotel window across
the street. He speaks into a walkie-talkie, and a car down
below pulls out to follow Helena.

                              ADLER
               Carl Ayala sits on the board of the
               Children's Hospital. He is heavily
               involved with Adult Literacy. He has a
               small boy and another child on the way.
                              (MORE)

                                                        (CONTINUED)

93   CONTINUED: 93

                          ADLER (cont'd)
              If you spread this kind of innuendo, you
              can expect legal recourse. Are we clear
              on this point?

                                                        CUT TO:

94   INT. GOVERNMENT BUILDING - EARLY MORNING   94

      The marble government corridors are empty. No one is in yet.
      One office has lights on.

95   INT. A.D.A. KELLY'S OFFICE - EARLY MORNING   95

      Robert Wakefield talks with an Assistant District Attorney,
      DAN KELLY, 40's.

                          ROBERT
              I appreciate you coming in so early.

                          A.D.A. KELLY
              Judge Wakefield, it's an honor to handle
              it for you. Consider it gone away. She's
              a minor; it probably would've expunged on
              her 18th birthday anyway.

                          ROBERT
              Still, this was a sensitive issue for me
              and I wanted to thank you personally.

                          A.D.A. KELLY
              Like I said, open container, P.I.,
              Misdemeanor possession. Easy to make it
              disappear. For you, poof, it's gone.

      A.D.A Kelly thinks a moment, then tries for tact.

                          A.D.A. KELLY (cont'd)
              One thing bothers me... That kid they
              dropped off had coke *and* heroin in him.
              Serious amounts. He's lucky he lived. So
              I gotta ask: what's your daughter on?

                          ROBERT
              I don't know what you mean.

                          A.D.A. KELLY
              I mean, did you ask her? What kind of
              drugs has she tried?

      Robert is silent for a beat.

                          ROBERT
              I... I don't really know.

                                                    (CONTINUED)

> A.D.A. KELLY
> Is she in any kind of therapy...
> professional help?

> ROBERT
> No, of course not. She's one of the top
> students at her school.

> A.D.A. KELLY
> Well, I hope it stays that way.

96   INT. ROBERT'S CAR - EARLY MORNING   96

Robert in his car, thinking. The streets are empty. He picks
up the cell phone.

> ROBERT
> (into phone)
> It's Robert. Wipe our schedule clean for
> the next three days. I'm tired of talking
> to experts who never set foot outside the
> beltway. It's time to see the front
> lines.

97   INT. CAROLINE WAKEFIELD'S BATHROOM - MORNING   97

Caroline sits on the toilet in her private bathroom. She's
not going to the bathroom, it's a seat and she's wearing her
pajamas. She's reading a magazine. The exhaust fan is on.

There are pictures of her and her friends on the walls:
goofy photos from camp, from school, a collage she's made
with cutouts from magazine pictures and copy.

On the sink next to her is a little square of well-charred
aluminum foil; she's done many hits. She leans over and picks
up a small piece of crack cocaine from a small pile in her
soap dish. She drops it on a clean place on the foil. She
picks up a lighter and the tube of a ball point pen she's
turned into a straw.

She heats the bottom of the foil. The crack "crackles." She
chases the smoke across the foil. A huge hit. She leans her
head back, her eyes roll back, she tries to focus on the
magazine, on anything, she stares up at the ceiling. She
holds it as long as she can then blows it toward the exhaust
fan.

Caroline looks at her watch. It's 7:20. She stands suddenly,
unsteadily. She looks at herself in the mirror. She's really
high and indecisive. She looks around wildly. She sees the
shower. She turns it on. She drops her pajamas.

97   CONTINUED: 97

She goes back to the foil and hits another piece of the rock,
taking another really big hit. She crushes the foil and
flushes it down the toilet. She hops in the shower.

98   IN THE SHOWER   98

The water streams over her face. After a long beat she
finally exhales the smoke of the hit through the water and
steam. She's in ecstacy.

It's almost time to leave for school.

                                                   CUT TO:

99   EXT. LA JOLLA PLAYGROUND - DAY   99

Helena reads a book, *Madame Bovary* by Gustave Flaubert, and
keeps an eye on David, who is playing on the monkey bars.

ACROSS THE ROAD at a careful distance is the ubiquitous
telephone repair van. On the roof a parabolic mike swivels
around.

100   INT. TELEPHONE REPAIR VAN - DAY   100

Castro and Gordon watch Helena via a small surveillance
monitor.

                    GORDON
          You should see little Montel play. Little
          Montel is the next Maradona.

                    CASTRO
          Maradona is a cokehead. Hand of God, my
          ass. We're wasting our time here.

                    GORDON
          He won. He was a winner. That bothers
          you.

                    CASTRO
          Winners don't do coke. Or haven't you
          been reading the bumper stickers?

Gordon looks at the monitor --

                    GORDON
          What do we have here?

ON THE MONITOR:

David kicking a soccer ball with an older strange man,
TIGRILLO, Latino, 40's, fit and tough looking.

                                                   (CONTINUED)

100 CONTINUED: 100

The man is very good. He juggles the ball and bounces it off
his head and David follows him away from the center of the
playground.

101 EXT. PLAYGROUND - CONTINUOUS   101

Helena notices David moving away while playing with the man.
She follows, then begins to jog after them.

                    HELENA
          David, come back here this minute. David!

As she closes distance the man stops juggling the ball and
abruptly picks up David and begins swinging him around by his
arms. David is having fun as Helena approaches.

                    HELENA (cont'd)
          David --

                    DAVID
          We're playing!

The strange man swings David up so that he's under his arm.

                    STRANGE MAN
          Yeah, this is fun.

                    HELENA
          Please put down my son.

The man holds David.

                    STRANGE MAN
          Shouldn't let your kid wander off with
          strangers.

                    HELENA
          Thank you. That's a valuable lesson.
          David, come on.

The strange man holds David tighter so that he's no longer
having fun. He begins to wriggle --

                    STRANGE MAN
          Mrs. Ayala --

This gets her attention --

                    STRANGE MAN (cont'd)
          Your husband owes a lot of money. Enough
          that snapping this kid's neck wouldn't
          nearly cover it.

David begins to cry. Helena looks around wildly for help.

                                            (CONTINUED)

101   CONTINUED: 101

                        STRANGE MAN (cont'd)
                You better come up with it in a hurry or
                your kid is going to disappear, and he
                won't turn up until the evening news.

He drops David who runs to his mother.

                        STRANGE MAN (cont'd)
                You get exactly one warning.

The strange man moves away across the field.

                        STRANGE MAN (cont'd)
                The first payment is three million
                dollars.

He continues walking away.

102   INT. TELEPHONE REPAIR VAN - DAY   102

Gordon and Castro stare with rapt attention.

                        GORDON
                Are you getting this on tape?

                        CASTRO
                I love my job. I love it. The next time
                I'm having a bad day you gotta remind me
                of right now and I'll get over it.

                                                        CUT TO:

A103   EXT. BARRACKS - NIGHT   A103

Javier and Manolo stand guard outside the front door of the
dining hall. Javi smokes a cigarette.

                        MANOLO
                A group of us are going out tonight.

                        JAVIER
                Who?

                        MANOLO
                Guzman, Tomas, Esteban --

                        JAVIER
                Your new friends.

                        MANOLO
                Yeah. It should be fun. You wanna come?

                                                        (CONTINUED)

                         JAVIER
              Not this time.

103 INT. DINING HALL - BARRACKS - NIGHT   103

     Francisco and Salazar eat at a beautifully set table. They
     are waited on by military officers who serve perfect flan at
     the end of the meal.

                         FRANCISCO
              In my home I have B&W speakers. I
              recently purchased a compact disc burner.
              I can make my own cd's, with whatever
              music I like, as if I bought them at the
              store, only I don't have to pay these
              crazy prices.

                         SALAZAR
              We have much in common. We both attended
              school in the United States, and both of
              our fathers are engineers.

                         FRANCISCO
              I got into stereo equipment when I was a
              kid. Some people don't notice the
              difference but it is very important to
              me.

                         SALAZAR
              Of course it is. Have some more wine.

     A soldier pours another glass of red for Francisco.

                         SALAZAR (cont'd)
              Now, Francisco, my friend... I must know
              where these men are who killed my
              captains. Not where they were last week,
              but where they are today, and better
              still, tomorrow. You are clever. You can
              predict where they will be, can't you?

     Francisco begins to weep.

     Salazar slides a pad of paper toward Francisco who slowly
     begins writing.

104 EXT. TIJUANA NEIGHBORHOOD - DAY   104

     Manolo and Javier pound on the front door of an apartment. A
     MAN opens the door and they grab him.

105   EXT. TIJUANA STREETS - DAY   105

A MAN walks down the street. Two SUV's pull up in front of
him. He starts to run. Salazar's men jump out and chase him.

Francisco is in the backseat of one of the SUV's, watching.

A106 EXT. TIJUANA - DAY   A106

An SUV pulls up to a curb.

B106 INT. SUV - DAY   B106

Javier and Manolo and Francisco sit in the SUV. Francisco is
weeping.

                    FRANCISCO
          I can't go home. I don't want to go.
          Please don't make me.

He looks beseechingly at them.

                    JAVIER
          It's not our decision.

                    FRANCISCO
          I'll be killed.

                    JAVIER
          Stop complaining. Nobody knows what
          you've been up to.

They push him out of the SUV.

                                            CUT TO:

106   INT. SAN DIEGO JAIL - DAY   106

Castro and Gordon sit with Eduardo Ruiz in a conference room.
They are recording his statements.

                    RUIZ
          Carlos, I mean Carl, started out in the
          family connection business: real estate
          in Tijuana, fishing boats out of
          Ensenada, hydroponic raspberries. He met
          up with the Obregon brothers of the
          Tijuana Cartel who were interested in two
          things: entering society and using his
          fishing boats.

                    GORDON
          So you pay off our customs officials?

                                            (CONTINUED)

> RUIZ
> In Mexico law enforcement is an
> entrepreneurial activity, this is not so
> true for the USA.
>   (condescending)
> Using regression analysis we made a study
> of the customs lanes at the border and
> calculated the odds of a search. The odds
> are not high, and we found variables that
> reduce the odds. We hire drivers with
> nothing to lose. Then we throw a lot of
> product at the problem. Some get stopped.
> Enough get through. It's not difficult.

> CASTRO
> You'd think he wasn't sitting here facing
> life in prison.

> RUIZ
> This has worked for years and it will
> continue to work for years. NAFTA makes
> everything more difficult for you. The
> border is disappearing.
>   (pointing at them)
> You people are like those Japanese
> soldiers left behind on deserted islands
> who think that World War II is still
> going on.
>   (with total disdain)
> Let me be the first to tell you, your
> government surrendered this war a long
> time ago.

> GORDON
>   (to Castro)
> This attitude's not gonna help him any,
> is it?

> RUIZ
> I got greedy. I decided to bring a little
> in on my own and somebody tipped you off.
> That was my mistake. Carl would never be
> so stupid.

> GORDON
> He hired you. That was a mistake.

> RUIZ
> Carl and I were friends from childhood.
> He was loyal, that's not a mistake.

107   EXT. TIJUANA - SAN DIEGO BORDER CROSSING - DAY   107

Car after car, an unending multi-lane stream of vehicles
moving into the U.S. Any of these cars could be carrying
drugs.

108   INT. CUSTOMS CONTROL BOOTH - DAY   108

On an elevated walkway, this booth commands a view of
everything. Robert and Sheridan listen to an OFFICIAL give
the spiel.

                    OFFICIAL
          The busiest land border crossing in the
          world. Over forty-one thousand vehicles
          per day, twenty-two thousand pedestrians
          on foot. I think we do a pretty good job
          but we know a lot of drugs are still
          getting through.

                    ROBERT
          Any idea how much?

                    OFFICIAL
          I've read official estimates but I
          wouldn't bet my house on them. I've heard
          the entire cocaine supply for the United
          States can fit into four tractor-
          trailers.
                    (gestures to the traffic)
          At least a half-dozen of those cars right
          out there are carrying a load of dope,
          with drivers employed by people who don't
          give a damn if they're caught or not.

                    ROBERT
          What do you look for?

                    OFFICIAL
          We ask questions and measure the answers.
          When something doesn't ring true, a fact
          that doesn't make sense, a slight
          hesitation, then it's off to secondary
          for a closer look. Before NAFTA we had
          about 1.9 million trucks a year. Now it's
          almost double. Pretty soon there'll be
          Mexican truck companies that will have as
          much freedom in crossing the border as
          American truck companies.

                    ROBERT
          Any way we can do it better?

                                        (CONTINUED)

                    OFFICIAL
          Sure. More money in intelligence on their
          side of the border. So we have a better
          idea who we're looking for. More dogs.
          More people. Supposed to be getting some
          giant x-ray machines to run the trucks
          through. Outside of martial law that's
          about the best you're gonna do.
                    (beat)
          But, I should tell you, there are two
          things that really have us on edge right
          now.
                    (beat)
          In the last six month seizures have
          tripled, even though we're pulling over
          the same number of cars. What does that
          tell you?

                    ROBERT
          That triple the amount of stuff is going
          through.

                    OFFICIAL
          Right. But, that's not the biggest
          problem. One of our Intel officers picked
          up information from DEA that traffickers
          have come up with a process, a chemical
          process, to turn coke into something
          else. It doesn't smell like coke. It
          doesn't look like coke. And what's worse,
          it doesn't react to field test. It could
          be anything. Maybe it's already
          happening. I mean, how would we know?

Robert looks out at the border activity. It's anarchy.

                                                    CUT TO:

109 INT. AYALA STUDY - AFTERNOON   109

Helena is on the floor surrounded by papers. She's made piles
of certain things: articles of incorporation,
shipping/transfer documentation, bank statements, credit card
statements. She holds a telephone to her ear --

                    HELENA
                 (into phone)
          Yes, hi Jenny, account number 4168 2245
          3173... I need a cash advance.

Helena walks into her kitchen. It's serene in the afternoon
light. She fixes ice-cold lemonade and fills two plastic
cups.

                                                    (CONTINUED)

109   CONTINUED: 109

                              HELENA (cont'd)
                    What's the largest amount I can get?
                         (listens)
                    Okay, I guess that'll have to do.

          Helena hangs up the phone. She takes the two cups of
          lemonade to the front door and steps outside.

110   EXT. AYALA HOME - AFTERNOON   110

          Helena carries the cups down the driveway. She presses a
          button and the gates swing open.

111   INT. TELEPHONE REPAIR VAN - AFTERNOON   111

          Gordon and Castro listen to their headsets. Suddenly --

                              VOICE (O.S.)
                         (over their headsets)
                    Okay. She's coming out. She's leaving her
                    property. Okay, she seems to be heading
                    for the van! She is approaching the van!

          Castro and Gordon look at each other.

                              GORDON
                    What do we do?

                              CASTRO
                    I don't know.

          There's a KNOCKING at the door of the van.

                              GORDON
                    What do you think she wants?

                              CASTRO
                    She's your girlfriend. Open it, talk
                    about your kids.

          Gordon opens the door. Helena is standing there with the
          lemonade.

                              HELENA
                    I so hope I didn't startle you. I thought
                    you might like some cold lemonade.

                              GORDON
                    Uh... Thank you.

          She hands the cups to him. Helena gathers herself.

                                                              (CONTINUED)

> HELENA
> I know this is a difficult situation and
> you're only doing your jobs. I don't bear
> you any ill-will, but I do have a small
> favor to ask.

> CASTRO
> You want to ask us a favor?

> HELENA
> A man threatened my children. These
> charges have attracted a lot of attention
> and it seems to be bringing all the nut-
> jobs out of the nut jar.
> (beat)
> Would you keep an eye out for anything
> out of the ordinary. I don't know what
> else to do.

> GORDON
> Of course, we will.

> HELENA
> Thank you.

They shut the door to the van and sit for a moment.

> CASTRO
> It's probably poisoned.

Gordon takes a big sip of his.

> GORDON
> It's good. Not too sweet.

CUT TO:

112   OMITTED   112

113   OMITTED   113

114   OMITTED   114

A115   EXT. TIJUANA STREET - MORNING   A115

This is a questionable neighborhood pushed up against the
edge of poverty.

Anna hurries across the street.

B115 EXT. JAVI'S APARTMENT BUILDING - MORNING   B115

Anna walks up the stairs of a rundown building. She passes
two PROSTITUTES loitering in the stairwell.

She knocks on a door and Javi, half-dressed for work,
answers. He's surprised to see her.

                    JAVIER
          Anna. What's wrong? What do you want?

                    ANNA
          I can't find Manolo.

                    JAVIER
          He's not here.

                    ANNA
          He never came home last night. Was he
          with you?

                    JAVIER
          No.

He lets her into the apartment.

C115 INT. JAVI'S APARTMENT - MORNING   C115

A small, clean room with a partition for the sleeping area.

                    ANNA
          I'm worried. Last time he was out late,
          I went through his clothes while he was
          asleep.

She pulls out a plastic packet with the scorpion insignia and
911 stamped on it.

Javier thinks a beat.

                    JAVIER
          I'll find him.

D115 EXT. ALLEY - TIJUANA - DAY   D115

Javi slams Manolo against the side of building.

                    JAVIER
          What the fuck are you doing? You're
          supposed to be at work. Look at you.

Manolo is sweaty and crazy-eyed.

                                              (CONTINUED)

D115 CONTINUED: D115

                              MANOLO
                    It's no problem. I was just with
                    everybody we work with.

                              JAVIER
                    Oh, really. General Salazar was there?

                              MANOLO
                    No, but a lot of other people. You should
                    come. You should come out with us.

                              JAVIER
                    Go home. Get cleaned up. Get to work.
                    Salazar is heading down to Mexico City
                    next week and I'm not getting left
                    behind. Don't fuck this up.

                                                       CUT TO:

EXT. COFFEE KIOSK - TIJUANA - DAY

Javi buys a cup of coffee. He turns. Two men, who will come
to be known as AGENT HUGHES and AGENT JOHNSON, are standing
close. Agent Hughes speaks without looking at him.

                              HUGHES
                    The word going around is you're not that
                    happy in your work.
                         (beat)
                    Maybe we can help.

Hughes sticks a business card in Javi's pocket. Javi watches
them walk away. It's all done so smoothly and quickly, it's
over before Javi even knows what happened.

115   EXT. WEST END - CINCINNATI - DAY   115

It's the bad part of urban Cincinnati in the daylight:
projects and blighted row houses. Seth and Caroline walk with
a slouched, alert air. In their mind's eye they are prep-
school gangsters following a familiar route.

                              SETH
                    You know my dad takes eight red cold
                    pills every day? He and my mom have
                    cocktail hour every night, from six to
                    seven, set your clock, two bourbons --

                              CAROLINE
                    Maybe we could show up and smoke a little
                    rock with them to unwind --

                                                   (CONTINUED)

                        SETH
Yeah, then some dope to take the edge off
at the end of a long day.

                  CAROLINE
Have you done your homework, honey?

                      SETH
Yes, mom --

                  CAROLINE
Then here's a little bump.

They turn down a street with a lot of activity on it.

                      SETH
Drugs weren't even a problem until a
hundred years ago when the white men in
power declared them a problem. Opiates.
But, who was using 'em? Chinese
immigrants. Slave labor. And the *darkies*
up in the inner cities dancing to them
evil rhythms of ju-ju music. People on
the fringe. Artists. *Decadent* rich
people. And who got scared? White men in
power. Who's scared today? White men in
power. If J.P. Morgan and John D.
Rockefeller ever admitted using, it'd be
a whole different story.

TWO YOUNG STREET DEALERS fall in step with them. One talks
without moving his lips --

                STREET DEALER
What you want?

                      SETH
911, and the come down.

One dealer hurries ahead toward the doorway of a falling-down
building.

                STREET DEALER
How much?

                      SETH
Two hundred of C, hundred of the other.

The dealer looks them over. He looks behind them down the
street.

                  CAROLINE
Come on... We've been here before.

                             (CONTINUED)

115   CONTINUED: (2)   115

                              STREET DEALER
                    Then, let's see your money.

Seth and Caroline are suspicious. They carefully show money
they both have in their front right pockets. The dealer
feints like he might grab it.

                         STREET DEALER (cont'd)
                    Up the steps. You the experts. You know
                    what to do.

They hurry up the steps into the dingy brownstone.

116   INT. ROW HOUSE - DAY   116

They step into the narrow foyer between the outer door and
the inner door. There are three other PEOPLE waiting
nervously. An older JUNKIE shoots them a crazy look --

                              JUNKIE
                    What are you two, about twelve?

                              CAROLINE
                    Fuck off.

They wait. Finally, the first dealer appears in the inner
door and lets them through.

117   INT. FIRST FLOOR CORRIDOR - DAY   117

They wait in a line in the narrow, poorly lit corridor. At
the end of the hall a hatch in a door slides back and the
drugstore is open. People buy and leave.

Seth and Caroline approach. In the hatch is a hardened
dealer, 20's, named SKETCH, which is tattooed on his forearm.
He checks out Caroline's body.

                              SETH
                    Caroline, give me your money.

She hands over her money to Seth who pays and gets the drugs:
gram baggies of rock stamped with a scorpion and **"911,"** and
wax-paper bindles of heroin, also labeled, **"911."**

Caroline has been watching the transaction. Sketch makes slow
eye contact with Caroline. After a beat --

                              SKETCH
                    Goodbye... Caroline.

Seth and Caroline make their way out of the building.

                                                    (CONTINUED)

117 CONTINUED: 117

                         SETH
                    (under his breath)
               Yeah, right.

118 EXT. BUILDING - DAY   118

     Seth and Caroline hold hands as they hurry down the steps.
     The lookout speaks without moving his lips.

                         STREET DEALER
               Now, get the fuck out of here.

     Caroline stops suddenly. She pulls Seth to her and kisses him
     hard. There's no better moment than the one right after
     scoring before you start using.

119 EXT. VILLA ELAINE - DAY   119

     A flophouse of the seediest variety: wino in the doorway,
     prostitutes taking care of business, everyone fresh out of
     institutions and graveyards.

120 INT. VILLA ELAINE - DAY   120

     They approach the front desk which is behind six inches of
     glass.

                         SETH
               We'd like room 205.

                         DESKMAN
               Then you hand me twenty-eight dollars.

121 INT. ROOM 205 - VILLA ELAINE - DAY   121

     They enter and the light bulb goes out. Seth fumbles his way
     to the mini-fridge, which he opens, throwing feeble light
     across the floor.

     They check out the decrepit room: the sloping mattress, the
     black and white television bolted to the bureau. The mini-
     fridge. Caroline bounces on the bed. They are teenagers. Seth
     prepares the drugs by the light of the mini-fridge.

                         SETH
               I love this place.

     Seth dumps the drugs on the bedside table. From other pockets
     he extracts aluminum foil, lighter, tube. She trails away
     watching him fix the first hit.

                                                        (CONTINUED)

>   SETH (CONT'D)
>   Did Courtney Love play Nancy in Syd and
>   Nancy?

>   CAROLINE
>   I think so. If she didn't she should
>   have.
>   (checks her watch)
>   I've only got maybe an hour. Then
>   volleyball practice is over and I have to
>   be home.

>   SETH
>   Why? Nobody's there.

He prepares the first hit. She does it and lies back. He does
one.

>   CAROLINE
>   (blowing out the hit)
>   The maid... They ask her what time I get
>   back. She spies for them.

Seth starts kissing her. They try to get into it, but both of
them are thinking about the drugs.

>   CAROLINE (cont'd)
>   I wish we could stay here. Just be here
>   forever and ever. Make it a little home.

She leans over to snort a tiny line of heroin.

>   SETH
>   I want to have sex and do a hit right as
>   we're coming.

Caroline's distracted by the line she's snorting. After a
while...

>   CAROLINE
>   Okay.

Seth begins undoing her jeans.

                                                            CUT TO:

122   INT. EPIC BUNKER LOBBY - DAY   122

SUPERTITLE: EL PASO, TEXAS

Robert and Sheridan listen to the official tour of the EPIC
center delivered by the SPECIAL-AGENT-IN-CHARGE, 40, a
sincere weight-lifter with a sincere crew-cut.

                                                        (CONTINUED)

122   CONTINUED: 122

                              SPECIAL-AGENT-IN-CHARGE
                    ... Over 200 DEA field agents, a budget
                    of almost 100 million dollars and state
                    of the art communications equipment make
                    the El Paso Information Center the Drug
                    Enforcement Administration's flagship for
                    the 21st century.

123   INT. EPIC BUNKER CAFETERIA - DAY   123

       A huge lunchroom. Long plastic institutional tables and
       agents minding their own business.

       Robert, Sheridan, and their Epic Guide walk through. They
       pass a wall of black and white head shots --

                              ROBERT
                    Who are these guys?

                              SPECIAL-AGENT-IN-CHARGE
                    Agents who died in the field.

124   EXT. BINOCULAR POV - DAY   124

       of a large mansion with manicured grounds. The back lawn is
       filled with children, balloons, a merry-go-round, and pony
       rides. It's a sumptuous children's birthday party.

                              SPECIAL-AGENT-IN-CHARGE
                    That house, that you see from the DEA
                    headquarters, belonged to Porfirio
                    Madrigal -- the Lord of the Skies,
                    largest trafficker in Mexico.

       ANGLE ON ROBERT

       looking through the binoculars.

                              ROBERT
                    He died in a liposuction surgery, right?

                              SPECIAL-AGENT-IN-CHARGE
                    Right. Now it's used by somebody from the
                    Juarez Cartel, one of his lieutenants...
                    Who knows?
                         (beat)
                    Every damn day there's a birthday party.
                    At first I thought they must have three
                    hundred children, then I realized they're
                    taunting us. Three miles away and we
                    can't touch them. Ha, ha, ha.

                                                              (CONTINUED)

124 CONTINUED: 124

BINOCULAR POV: a child running in circles holding a clutch of colored balloons.

> ROBERT
> Who do we interface with on their side?

> SPECIAL-AGENT-IN-CHARGE
> What do you mean?

> ROBERT
> I mean, who runs interdiction on the
> Mexico side?

> SPECIAL-AGENT-IN-CHARGE
> I don't know. I don't think there's any
> one person.
>> (thinks)
> See the problem is the Juarez cartel owns
> everything and everybody, all the
> property on the Mexican side, sometimes
> all the property on both sides.
> Warehouses, transportation, even tunnels.
> It's very organized.

125 EXT. TARMAC - DAY   125

Robert, walking with purpose, leads his group to their plane.

126 INT. MILITARY JET - DAY   126

Robert and Sheridan and several DEA, Law Enforcement, and Military Officials. It's a nice plane, used for important people and Robert has the best seat.

> ROBERT
> I want everyone thinking out the box for
> a second. What are we gonna do about
> Mexico?
>> (silence)
> Come on, guys. Out of the box.

The men on the plane just stare at him. Finally the REP FROM DEA leans forward.

> REP FROM DEA
> Unlimited funds?

> ROBERT
> Unlimited.

> REP FROM DEA
> From a DEA standpoint we need a vetted
> task force and matching funds.
>> (MORE)

(CONTINUED)

126   CONTINUED: 126

                          REP FROM DEA (cont'd)
            And cut the red tape on getting them
            equipment and training.

Robert turns to the others.

                          ROBERT
            Come on. I want to hear from everyone:
            FBI. Customs. Treatment. Is there anyone
            from treatment on this plane?
                    (no one answers)
            Then I want an answer for why there isn't
            anyone from treatment.
                    (beat)
            Look, we know we have to bust one of
            these cartels, Juarez or Tijuana, not
            just as a symbol, but hell yes, also as a
            symbol - they are symbols - and there's
            nothing wrong with sending a message.
            That's why when Carlos Ayala hired
            Michael Adler lead defense, I flew Ben
            Williams to San Diego to prosecute.
            Because he's the best we have, he's our
            symbol that we're serious about putting
            the top people away.
                    (beat)
            So, as of right now, this flight only,
            consider the dam on new ideas thrown
            open.

Still, no one else says anything. They watch Robert
impassively.

                          ROBERT (cont'd)
            If I'm not mistaken, we got DEA,
            Pentagon, U.S. Attorneys office, about a
            billion dollars of budget right here. So
            what are you people waiting for?

                                                 CUT TO:

127   OMITTED   127

128   EXT. SAN DIEGO OFFICE BUILDING - DAY   128

Establishing shot of a tall glass building in the downtown
skyline of San Diego.

129   INT. ARNIE METZGER'S OFFICE - DAY   129

Helena and Arnie enter his office. The furniture is sleek mid-
century modern, and the view of the harbor is extraordinary.

                          ARNIE
            On a clear day you can see Mexico City.

                                              (CONTINUED)

Arnie stands very close to Helena and looks at her profile.

                    ARNIE (cont'd)
          This place is swept twice a day. I
          learned that in Miami in '85. Then the
          U.S. shut down the whole Caribbean, but
          it's a big game of wack-a-mole. Knock it
          down in Miami, it pops up here. And San
          Diego is so much more relaxing.

                    HELENA
          Arnie, I need money. Somebody threatened
          my children. They want a first payment of
          three million dollars.

                    ARNIE
          Helena, if I had it I would give it to
          you, but I don't have that kind of money.

                    HELENA
          Arnie, help me. Doesn't anyone owe us
          money?

                    ARNIE
          Yes, I told you before, there are people
          who owe you money but they're not paying.
          There's too much heat on Carl.

                    HELENA
          Please. Tell me who Carl sells to.

Arnie thinks.

                    ARNIE
          Even if I knew I wouldn't tell you. You
          do not want to come into contact with
          these people. Only Carl knows who they
          are. That's his real asset. Ruiz doesn't
          know them. They don't know Ruiz. Church
          and State.

                    HELENA
          What about legitimate businesses? We own
          a construction concern, real estate --

                    ARNIE
          Laundromats for the washing of money.
          Unfortunately, Carl had only one
          successful business.

                    HELENA
          Don't you have some good news? Isn't
          there something positive you could say.

                                              (CONTINUED)

There isn't. Helena looks Arnie in the eyes.

> HELENA (CONT'D)
> (vulnerable)
> Sometimes I wonder what I'll do if Carl
> doesn't get out. I'm not very adept at
> being on my own. I've always had a man in
> my life. Always.

> ARNIE
> I remember when I first met you: little
> Helen Watts from the wrong side of
> somewhere. I had a feeling even then that
> your survival instincts were pretty well
> honed.

> HELENA
> I'm glad you think so, but I'm picturing
> a debt-ridden, thirty-two year-old mother
> whose ex-husband is being compared to
> Pablo Escobar.
> (beat)
> And I'm wondering who would want to be
> with someone like that?

It takes a great effort for Arnie not to answer.

                                                          CUT TO:

A130 OMITTED   A130

131   OMITTED   131

132   OMITTED   132

133   OMITTED   133

134   OMITTED   134

A135 INT. ARMORED SUV - MEXICO - DAY   A135

Javier and Manolo ride through a nice neighborhood in Mexico
City. Javi isn't familiar with the roads and drives
cautiously.

A young lady, ROSARIO, early 20's, sexy and vulnerable, rides
in the back of the SUV.

> ROSARIO
> You two don't like me, do you?

Manolo laughs and looks her up and down. Javi watches her in
the rearview mirror.

                                                    (CONTINUED)

> JAVIER
> We don't have an opinion on you.

> ROSARIO
> (to Javi)
> Maybe it's because I'm getting an
> apartment nicer than anything you'll ever
> see in your life?

Javi says nothing.

> ROSARIO (cont'd)
> (re: the neighborhood)
> I can't believe the old man kept his
> promise.

> JAVIER
> The General is a man of his word.

> ROSARIO
> They will say anything to get what they
> want, but then you remind them, it's
> always tomorrow, tomorrow, tomorrow.
> (beat)
> Occupational hazard, I guess.

Javi just looks at her in the rearview mirror.

> ROSARIO (CONT'D)
> His friend is giving us the apartment so
> it's not like he paid. It's more like a
> favor.

Javier pulls the SUV to the curb in front of a beautiful
colonial-style apartment complex in the verdant neighborhood.

B135 EXT. VERDANT NEIGHBORHOOD - DAY   B135

Birds are chirping. Javi waits in the car as Manolo takes the
young lady's bags from the vehicle and carries them up the
walkway to the arched doorway. He knocks on the heavy wooden
door.

> ROSARIO
> You don't have the keys. Oh that's
> perfect. Are you an idiot?

Manolo knocks again. They wait a long beat.

> MANOLO
> There's supposed to be someone here to
> let you in.

B135 CONTINUED: B135

Finally, the door swings open and a BODYGUARD is standing
there. Rosario SQUEALS and sweeps past him into the vast
space. The bodyguard motions for Manolo to put the bags
inside the door.

Manolo sets the bags down and sees another MAN standing a few
feet away. The man wears sunglasses. His complexion is
strange and his neck is bandaged.

The body guard escorts Manolo back outside where he hears
Rosario's happy LAUGHTER drifting down from an upstairs
window.

C135 INT. SUV - DAY   C135

Manolo gets into the truck. He's shaken by what he's just
seen.

                    MANOLO
          Madrigal's alive.

                    JAVIER
          What?

                    MANOLO
          Porfirio Madrigal is not dead. I just saw
          him.

A long beat as Javier considers this.

                    JAVIER
          This is why Salazar is so interested in
          cleaning up Tijuana. Madrigal, who's
          supposed to be dead, owns him. And
          Madrigal is making a move on Juan
          Obregon.

Javier calmly drives away.

                    MANOLO
          Javi! Come on. Don't pull this you don't
          care bullshit. This is incredible
          information. It must be. Javi --

                    JAVIER
          We keep our mouths shut.

                                              CUT TO:

135   INT. BARBARA'S CAR - NIGHT   135

Barbara drives Robert home from the airport. There's a sense
they've been silent for a while.

                                              (CONTINUED)

>   ROBERT
>   I think we may have found our Mexican
>   Drug Czar. It's this General, Salazar. At
>   least I'll have somebody on the other
>   side I can talk to.

>   BARBARA
>   Does this mean you're going to be gone
>   more?

A long silence.

>   ROBERT
>   Possibly.

Another silence.

>   BARBARA
>   You might want to pencil in a little *face-
>   time* with your daughter.

>   ROBERT
>   Barbara --

>   BARBARA
>   Because I'm at the edge of my
>   capabilities, Robert.

>   ROBERT
>   The first thing we have to do is present
>   a unified front.

>   BARBARA
>   If you start in on the war metaphors I'm
>   going to drive this car into a fucking
>   telephone pole.

>   ROBERT
>   Look, I'm as worried as you are --

>   BARBARA
>   No, I don't think so. *Leave me alone,
>   give me money.* That's what I get from our
>   daughter. She has a way of shutting me
>   out that seems very familiar.

>   ROBERT
>   Yeah, well, she has a way of self-
>   medicating that probably seems familiar,
>   too.

She looks at him, stung.

                                            (CONTINUED)

135   CONTINUED: (2)   135

                         BARBARA
               I'm not the one who has to have three
               scotches just to walk in the door and say
               hello.

                         ROBERT
               I have a drink before dinner to take the
               edge off my day. That's different.

                         BARBARA
               Oh, it is?

                         ROBERT
               Yeah, because the alternative is to be
               bored to death.

136   EXT. WAKEFIELD HOUSE - NIGHT   136

      The car pulls into the driveway. Robert gets out. Barbara
      doesn't. He looks back at her.

                         BARBARA
               Why don't you go in and tell your
               daughter how bored you are.

      She puts the car in reverse and drives away. He stands for a
      moment, steaming.

137   INT. WAKEFIELD HOUSE - NIGHT   137

      Robert Wakefield steps inside his home. It's very QUIET. He
      checks the mail on the hall table.

138   INT. UPSTAIRS HALLWAY - NIGHT   138

      Robert walks down the hallway. He steps into Caroline's
      bedroom.

139   INT. CAROLINE WAKEFIELD'S BEDROOM - CONTINUOUS   139

      Robert stands outside her closed bathroom door.

      There is nothing, then from the other side of the door, the
      faint sound of a lighter CLICKING. AGAIN and AGAIN, then a
      COUGH.

140   INT. CAROLINE WAKEFIELD'S BATHROOM - NIGHT   140

      Caroline sits on the toilet. Glamour Magazine on her lap.
      She's wild-eyed and paranoid. The exhaust fan is running. The
      aluminum foil is on the sink. The last little bit of heroin
      in a wax-paper bundle sits beside it.

She's listening hard for any SOUND in the house. What she's
wondering is if someone is outside the door listening.

She puts a piece of crack on the foil and listens hard once
more before lighting it. She does the hit. And seems to feel
better.

Suddenly there's a POUNDING on the door. The VOICE of her
father muffled through the solid wood.

                    ROBERT (V.O.)
               (muffled by the door)
          Caroline. Open this door immediately.

Caroline is up like a shot. She looks around. The POUNDING on
the door gets stronger.

She crumples the foil and drops it in the toilet.

The bathroom door SOUNDS like it's about to cave inward.

                    CAROLINE
               (faking the best she can)
          Who is it? I'm going to the bathroom.

She's coping now, full parallel process mode: she dumps the
last heroin on the back of her hand and snorts it, checking
her nose in the mirror as she reaches for a can of air
freshener which she sprays into the air.

                    CAROLINE (cont'd)
          One minute.

She takes the remaining crack, lighters, tubes, little smudgy
druggy bits of paraphernalia and carefully places it all in a
hiding place above the bathroom cabinet.

She pauses a beat, then opens the door, and tries to brush by
her father while avoiding his eyes.

                    CAROLINE (cont'd)
          Excuse me --

Robert grabs her by the arms. He pushes her against the wall
and looks at her pupils. He looks at her fingernails. The
blister on her thumb from working the lighter is red and
irritated.

                    ROBERT
          You're not going anywhere, young lady.

She stands there; she's very high.

                                              (CONTINUED)

Robert sniffs the air. He throws open cabinets, searching for drugs. He sees the smudge mark on the counter left by the charred aluminum foil.

>   ROBERT (cont'd)
>   Where is it? Where are the drugs?
>   (yelling)
>   Where are they?

>   CAROLINE
>   Fuck you. I wasn't doing anything.
>   You're like the Gestapo.

Robert KICKS the cabinets.

>   ROBERT
>   Fuck me? Oh, okay. Fuck me. Fuck you.

Robert is losing it. He throws stuff around the bathroom

and then, for the first time, looks up. He sees the long light in the box atop the medicine cabinet and it dawns on him.

>   ROBERT (cont'd)
>   I'm going to ask you one time to tell me
>   the truth so that I can help you.

She just stares.

>   ROBERT (CONT'D)
>   Okay, young lady, that's it.

>   CAROLINE
>   Like I give a fuck.

Robert reaches above the medicine cabinet and pulls out a charred spoon. It confuses him. He throws it into the sink.

He pulls out another spoon. He pulls out crumpled bindles, rolled up, encrusted dollar bills, exhausted lighters, a pill bottle, an empty pint of vodka.

The detritus of drug addiction keeps on coming, filling up the sink. Robert stares at it, the amount and complexity has him momentarily baffled.

>   ROBERT
>   What is wrong with you? What?
>   (beat)
>   You're going away. You're getting help
>   somewhere.

140   CONTINUED: (3)   140

                    CAROLINE
           You can't make me.

                    ROBERT
           Oh, yes I can.

                                                   CUT TO:

141   OMITTED   141

142   OMITTED   142

143   OMITTED   143

A144 INT. - SAN DIEGO - DAY   A144

      Javier drives toward downtown. He's sipping a Burger King
      soft-drink. On the seat next to him is a shopping bag from
      Target. He takes an exit. Javier pulls into the underground
      parking lot of a fancy office tower.

B144 INT. POLICE SEDAN - DAY   B144

      Javi drives down to the third floor underground. He pulls
      into a parking spot next to a white sedan. He slides open the
      cargo door of his van.

      The cargo door of the sedan opens. Javi quickly gets into the
      sedan.

C144 INT. SEDAN - DAY   C144

      Special Agents Hughes and Johnson welcome Javi.

                    JAVIER
           Where are we going?

      Hughes sticks out his hand.

                    HUGHES
           Special Agent Hughes, Drug Enforcement
           Administration of the United States.

                    JAVIER
                (ignoring the niceties)
           Where are you taking me?

      The agents exchange a look.

                    JOHNSON
           Somewhere safe.

                                            (CONTINUED)

C144 CONTINUED: C144

                    JAVIER
          Where?

                    JOHNSON
          A place we have, that we know is
          protected.

                    JAVIER
          No.

                    HUGHES
          It's really safe.

                    JAVIER
          Not for me.

                    JOHNSON
          Okay. Where would you like to go?

D144 EXT. SWIMMING POOL - HOTEL - DAY   D144

     Javi and Agents Johnson and Hughes stand in the middle of the
     shallow end of a large swimming pool. KIDS in waterwings
     splash nearby.

                    JAVIER
          It's important that we work together.
          Mexico. America. One hand washing the
          other.

                    JOHNSON
          We agree.

                    JAVIER
          So... maybe you tell me about your
          informants in our operations.

                    JOHNSON
               (confused by this)
          We thought maybe you'd have that kind of
          information for us.

                    JAVIER
               (feigning surprise)
          This is a very different proposition.

     Johnson and Hughes exchange a glance.

                    JOHNSON
          We pay for that kind of information.

     A fat kid in an inner-tube floats behind them.

(CONTINUED)

D144 CONTINUED: D144

                    JOHNSON (CONT'D)
          Is that what you're talking about,
          Javier?

Javi makes eye contact with one agent, then the other.

                    JAVIER
          Ten years ago Tijuana had no drug
          problem. Now it is epidemic.
             (beat)
          Ten years ago America takes a hammer to
          Pablo Escobar, a hammer to the Miami drug
          trade, and you allowed everything to move
          to my country. You dumped the problem at
          our feet. Now, drug use is epidemic. Now,
          the treatment centers are full and get no
          state money. They survive on donations
          and what they get for building doghouses
          to sell to the U.S.
             (beat)
          We need lights for the parks so kids can
          play at night. So they can play baseball.
          So it's safe. Everybody likes parks.
          Everybody likes baseball.
             (beat)
          What I'm talking about is I would like to
          see somebody take an interest in Tijuana.
          That's what I'm talking about.

Javi starts to get out of the pool.

                    HUGHES
          Javi, You want to come see us again,
          you're going on the box. No more of this
          water-wing bullshit.

E144 INT. PARKING GARAGE - DAY   E144

Javier gets out of the DEA sedan and back into his. He drives
away.

F144 INT. SEDAN - DAY   F144

Agent Hughes turns to Agent Johnson.

                    JOHNSON
          You wanna tell me what the hell that was
          all about?

> HUGHES
> He's got something. We just have to be
> patient.

CUT TO:

144   INT. JAIL VISITATION ROOM - DAY   144

Helena and Carl each hold a telephone receiver as they stare
at each other through a thick pane of meshed glass. Helena is
barely holding it together. It's hard for Carl to see her
like this. After a beat --

> CARL
> How's David?

> HELENA
> How's David? *How's David?* He's terrific,
> Carl.

> CARL
> Helena --

> HELENA
> He watched his father get dragged away by
> federal agents. I don't even know how to
> begin to tell him where you are or when
> you're coming back... Or if you're coming
> back.

She can't even look at him.

> CARL
>   (beat)
> We'll get through this, I promise. I'll
> make it up to you --

> HELENA
>   (snapping)
> How? Supportive letters from prison while
> I'm being kicked out of our home?
>   (beat)
> Do you have any idea what is happening
> out here? Our credit cards are maxed. The
> people at the bank, you should see their
> faces when I walk in there. I have a
> letter from the government telling me
> that anything I sell from our house will
> be taken against an income tax lien. Our
> friends are behaving like the crowd at a
> public hanging. Nobody will help us.
> Nobody will take us in. Nobody wants
> anything to do with us.
>   (MORE)

                              HELENA (cont'd)
                    So tell me, Carl, how you're gonna make
                    it up to me.
                              (losing it)
                    Tell me again how we'll get through this,
                    and maybe while you're at it you can put
                    your hand up against the glass so we can
                    have a tender moment of connection.

                              CARL
                    Helena --

                              HELENA
                    Tell me what to do, Carl. I need
                    guidance, not a fucking platitude.
                              (beat)
                    I'm not bringing a child into the kind of
                    life I grew up with. I won't do it. I
                    want our life back.

Carl looks at his wife as if he is trying to weigh her. He
thinks, then leans forward --

                              CARLOS
                    I built our house and I don't want to
                    lose it. Every stone, every brick, every
                    board.
                              (carefully)
                    My business... That would take a lot of
                    private study...
                              (he blinks)
                    That you don't have time for. I suggest
                    you look into the Coronel...
                              (he blinks again)
                    Into selling it. If you can stomach it,
                    you should look into it. That painting is
                    very valuable.

                              HELENA
                    I don't understand.

                              CARLOS
                    Look into the Coronel; otherwise, there
                    is nothing to do.

                                                            CUT TO:

145   EXT. SERENITY OAKS - DAY   145

      A peaceful wooded campus with a unobtrusive sign reading,
      "Serenity Oaks Treatment Facility."

146   INT. MEETING ROOM - SERENITY OAKS - DAY   146

There are sayings on the walls: "Easy Does It;" "Let Go and
Let God;" "Turn it over;" "One Day at a Time..." "H.A.L.T. --
Hungry? Angry? Lonely? Tired?"

Caroline, wearing a thick, woolly sweater, and the other
PATIENTS sit around on beat-up couches and chairs in a loose
circle. It's a mixed BUNCH: trucker meth-head, rocker dope-
fiend, yuppie crack-head, fat, thin, rich, middle-class, and
all white. Caroline is the youngest.

MARTY, 40's, an overweight alcoholic, finishes his "share."

                    MARTY
          ... So it was my birthday and my ex-wife
          was getting remarried and I was in some
          church basement telling a bunch of
          strangers how it was a good day because I
          didn't have to eat out of a dumpster.
          That was enough to send me out on big
          one.
               (beat)
          I've been thinking a lot about the first
          step: that I came to believe I was
          powerless over alcohol and that my life
          had become unmanageable.
               (beat)
          See my disease tells me I don't have a
          disease. That I'm fine. That it's my
          birthday and I can have one little drink,
          then one little line, then one little
          Valium, then two more fat lines, then two
          more 10 mil Valium... Six months later I
          wake up in a sober living house in
          Philly. And I'm from Dallas, people.
               (beat)
          It's a disease -- an allergy of the body
          and an obsession of the mind. I know that
          now. So my name's Marty and today I'm a
          grateful recovering alcoholic who didn't
          eat out of a dumpster. Thanks.

And Marty looks to Caroline who didn't relate to one word he
said.

                    CAROLINE
               (slowly, very nervous)
          Hi. I'm Caroline. I'm not sure I'm an
          alcoholic.
               (beat)
          I mean I don't really like to drink.
               (MORE)

                                              (CONTINUED)

146   CONTINUED: 146

                         CAROLINE (cont'd)
          For someone my age it's so much easier to
          get drugs than beer. I don't know, this
          is really weird and I'm really nervous...

People in the room nod encouragingly.

                         CAROLINE (cont'd)
          I guess I'm angry. I mean I think I'm
          really angry about a lot of stuff, but I
          don't know what exactly.

She blushes, and stares out the window.

                                                        CUT TO:

147   INT. AYALA LIVING ROOM - AFTERNOON   147

Helena follows an ART APPRAISER through her formal living
room as he inspects paintings and makes notations. He is very
excited and moves quickly from one to the next.

                         ART APPRAISER
          Tamayo. Carrington. A simply wonderful
          collection of Mexican Modern. Give me
          three months. I know several collectors
          in South America, very discreet.

                         HELENA
          I don't have three months.

                         ART APPRAISER
          It takes time to find the proper
          collection.

                         HELENA
          How much will you give me in cash? Today.

The appraiser taps out some numbers on a calculator and shows
the figure to Helena.

                         HELENA (cont'd)
          You must be joking. That's a fraction of
          their value.

                         ART APPRAISER
          I'm sorry, but that is the figure I can
          get today.

Helena turns her back. She walks to a window and looks out,
then surveys the contents of her beautiful home.

                         HELENA
              (snapping)
          Get out. Get out of my house.

                                                  (CONTINUED)

147   CONTINUED: 147

Helena turns and sees David in the doorway. She goes to him.

                    HELENA (cont'd)
              It's all right. We're having a
              disagreement, that's all.

The art appraiser passes them on his way out.

148   INT. AYALA MASTER BEDROOM - NIGHT   148

Helena wakes up in the middle of the night with a start. Her
eyes are wide open. She has had a thought --

She climbs out of bed and quickly puts on a robe.

149   INT. UPSTAIRS HALLWAY - CONTINUOUS   149

Helena walks quickly and quietly down the hallway. She passes
David's room. She opens a door at the end of the hall --

150   INT. CARL'S PRIVATE STUDY - CONTINUOUS   150

Helena enters the room. She hits a desk lamp and we're in a
very comfortable and masculine upstairs study: bookshelves
holding hundreds of art books; comfortable chairs; MacIntosh
stereo; discreet flatscreen HD TV.

Helena stares at a painting on one of the bookshelves. It is
"Boy with a Hoop," a small portrait by Rafael Colonel.

She goes to it and looks from different angles. She reaches
out and jiggles the oil. Nothing happens. She looks behind
the painting at the backing.

She notices that one corner is not glued down. She picks up a
letter opener and pries the paper back. An envelope slips
out.

Inside the envelope: neat, thin strips of paper dense with
information in a miniscule type and a magnetic key card.

                                                    CUT TO:

151   OMITTED   151

152   OMITTED   152

153   OMITTED   153

A154   INT. HELICOPTER - DAY   A154

Robert and Sheridan ride in the back of the chopper. Each
looks out his own window.

                                              (CONTINUED)

A154 CONTINUED: A154

A newspaper on the seat between them shows a front page photo
of General Salazar, exultant, and the headline reads in
Spanish, "Salazar Named Chief of Anti-Narcotics Operations."

B154 EXT. MEXICO CITY - DAY   B154

Establishing shot of a military helicopter landing on the
roof of an office building in downtown Mexico City.

C154 INT. HEADQUARTERS, FEADS, - MEXICO CITY - DAY   C154

Robert Wakefield and General Salazar stroll through the new
headquarters where boxes are still being unpacked. Javier and
Sheridan trail along behind them.

                    SALAZAR
          I recruited the best men in Mexico for my
          task force and put them through a
          rigorous screening process. Not only
          physical, but also psychological.

                    ROBERT
          I'd like to bring you up to Washington,
          walk you around our side of things, and
          share some of the information we've been
          able to develop on your cartels.

                    SALAZAR
          That would be very helpful to me.
               (beat)
          Also, I received the offer from DEA and
          the FBI to train some of my men at
          Quantico. I think this will be extremely
          useful, a good way for us to absorb some
          of your methods.

D154 INT. SALAZAR'S I.N.C.D. OFFICE - DAY   D154

The office hasn't been decorated yet.

                    SALAZAR
          I've been too busy to completely settle
          in.

Salazar proffers a chair and they sit next to each other like
Brezhnev and Nixon. PHOTOGRAPHERS begin SNAPPING pictures.
After a few moments, Salazar waves them away, and they lower
their cameras and leave.

                    ROBERT
          You've been making very good progress
          against the Tijuana cartel.

                                            (CONTINUED)

> SALAZAR
> Yes, I am confident that Juan Obregon
> will be taken into custody before the end
> of the year. But, you must understand
> that it is very difficult because of
> corruption in the police force. We get a
> tip that he is one place, then we get
> there and he is already gone, having been
> warned by someone on our side.

> ROBERT
> Hopefully the exchange of training
> methods and information between our
> countries will help with this problem.

> SALAZAR
> Yes, I hope so as well.

> ROBERT
> Let me ask you a related question. We've
> talked about the supply side, but what
> about demand? What is your policy for
> treating addiction?

> SALAZAR
> Addicts treat themselves... they overdose
> and then there's one less to worry about.

Robert cannot respond.

                                                        CUT TO:

154   EXT. SERENITY OAKS - WALKWAY - DAY   154

Caroline ambles alone down a walkway at the treatment
facility.

She looks through the trees that surround the facility and
notices cars going by.

                                                        CUT TO:

155   INT. LOW-RENT HOTEL - DAY   155

Gordon and another DEA AGENT escort Ruiz up the stairs of a
large, older hotel.

> RUIZ
> This is ridiculous. Why is there no
> elevator?

                                                        (CONTINUED)

155   CONTINUED: 155

                          GORDON
               When the DEA gets into the narcotics
               business, then we'll stay at the Four
               Seasons.

They walk down a hotel hallway. Two more AGENTS stand outside
Room 407. Gordon opens the door and they enter.

156   INT. SUITE OF CHEAP HOTEL ROOMS - DAY   156

There are more AGENTS inside and old food and coffee
containers. Gordon gives Ruiz a tour. There are several
rooms. A bored Castro sits at a table staring at a Scrabble
board.

                          CASTRO
               Eddie, how you like your new home? I hope
               you hate it as much as I do.

Ruiz looks around with disgust. He's accustomed to finer
places. He goes to a window and looks out.

RUIZ'S POV: of the Federal Court building not far away.

                          RUIZ
               This is not what my lawyers negotiated.

Gordon pours himself a cup of coffee.

                          GORDON
               Fuck your lawyers. You aren't getting any
               cappuccino or Biscotti either.

157   INT. FEDERAL COURTHOUSE - DAY   157

A packed, tense courtroom listens to testimony from a
government witness, FRANK, 50's, very matter-of-fact and
truthful.

                          FRANK
               He first came to me in January. That
               would've been nineteen eighty-seven. He
               wanted to rent warehouse space along the
               harbor. I didn't ask too many questions;
               I'm a businessman also.

158   INT. FEDERAL COURTHOUSE - DAY   158

Another witness, MRS. BERRY, 40's, pedantic on the stand --

                          MRS. BERRY
               I told Mr. Ayala there were
               irregularities in his tax return.
                          (MORE)

                                              (CONTINUED)

158   CONTINUED: 158

                          MRS. BERRY (cont'd)
                 And I couldn't represent him unless we
                 could explain this...

159   INT. FEDERAL COURTHOUSE - DAY   159

      SHEILA, 38, a mousy secretary, is on the stand. Carlos sits
      at the defendant's table listening raptly. Gordon and Castro
      sit in the back watching Helena who pays close attention to
      the witness --

                          SHEILA
                 I was the company secretary from 1991 to
                 1994. I supposedly worked for all six
                 companies. But... they weren't... I mean,
                 it was just one empty office with a desk
                 and a telephone. We never sold anything
                 the whole time I was there. Sometimes
                 people came and got paid. I don't really
                 know what we did.

                          PROSECUTOR
                 Did Mr. Ayala say where the money came
                 from?

                          SHEILA
                 No, and I didn't ask.

                          PROSECUTOR
                 Where do you think it came from?

      Carl's lawyer, Adler, is on his feet --

                          KAUFMAN
                 This is speculation --

                          PROSECUTOR
                 I'll rephrase. Did you feel like you were
                 engaged in a legal enterprise?

      Sheila is reluctant to answer.

                          SHEILA
                 No, not really.

      Helena catches Carl's eye and they share a grim moment.

                                                          CUT TO:

160   OMITTED   160

161   OMITTED   161

162   OMITTED   162

163 OMITTED   163

164 INT. CARL'S UPSTAIRS STUDY - DAY   164

Helena sits at Carl's office desk. On the desk in front of
her are the lists she found and an encrypted cell phone.

Helena picks up the phone. Her hands are shaking. She is
crying as she dials. A voice on the other end answers.

                    FRANCISCO (V.O.)
               Who is this?

Helena gathers her courage, then...

                    HELENA
               A friend... of Carlos Ayala.

There is a long pause.

                    FRANCISCO (V.O.)
               Yes.

                    HELENA
               I'm on a special phone, may I speak
               freely?

                    FRANCISCO (V.O.)
               You may speak.

                    HELENA
               I have a job for you and I don't have
               much time.

165 EXT. BOTANICAL GARDEN - DAY   165

Helena watches David look at the wide variety of plants and
flowers. All around them a GROUP of 3rd graders, in identical
T-shirts, enjoy a field trip.

                    FRANCISCO (V.O.)
               I love this place. Don't turn around.

Behind her Francisco Flores takes a photo with an instant
camera.

                    FRANCISCO (cont'd)
               You were followed by the police, but they
               won't hear us over the children. I want
               to use a bomb.

(CONTINUED)

                    HELENA
          You're kidding. Can't you shoot him or
          something?

                    FRANCISCO
          I don't really like guns. You shoot
          someone in the head three times and some
          doctor will keep them alive.

                    HELENA
          When will you do it?

                    FRANCISCO
          I don't know. Eduardo Ruiz is the only
          real witness against Carl. The security
          is very tight. There may not be a way.

                    HELENA
          There's always a way. If people get to
          the Pope or the President, you can get to
          him.

Francisco laughs.

                    FRANCISCO
          Careful... You're sounding like your
          husband, Mrs. Ayala.

                                                        CUT TO:

166   OMITTED   166

167   OMITTED   167

A168 INT. JAVI'S APARTMENT - NIGHT   A168

Anna sits in the living room, staring. She appears too upset
to speak. The apartment is cleaner. There have been other
changes. There's a new rug.

                    JAVIER
          What? What is it?

                    ANNA
          It's very hard for me to come and tell
          you this.

Javier just watches her.

                    ANNA (cont'd)
          It's Manolo. He's going to do something
          stupid. I'm worried that he'll get
          himself killed.

                                                    (CONTINUED)

He keeps watching.

                    ANNA (cont'd)
          He's saying he's going to talk to the
          Americans. Become an informer. He says
          they pay a lot of money.

                    JAVIER
          Why does he need money?

                    ANNA
          He has debts. He has gambling debts. He
          owes a lot of money.

                    JAVIER
          How much?

                    ANNA
          Nine thousand dollars.

A long beat.

                    JAVIER
          What is he planning on telling them?

                    ANNA
          Well, you know, he's going to say about
          Madrigal... and Salazar.

Javier just looks at her.

                                                     CUT TO:

168   INT. ROBERT'S OFFICE IN WASHINGTON - DAY   168

      Robert is on the telephone, listening. He is not happy.
      Sheridan watches him.

                    ROBERT
                  (into phone)
          Nobody saw her leave?
                  (beat)
          Yes... I understand.

      He hangs up. He stands and reaches for his jacket.

                    ROBERT (cont'd)
          I have to go. I have to go home.

169   INT. WAKEFIELD KITCHEN - NIGHT   169

      Robert and Barbara sit at the kitchen table.

                                                     (CONTINUED)

169   CONTINUED: 169

> BARBARA
> Should we bring the police into this?

> ROBERT
> No, not yet.

170   EXT. WEST END STREETS - DAY   170

Robert drives through the streets in his Cadillac DeVille.

171   INT. DEVILLE - DAY   171

Robert rides in glum silence. He looks at passersby who are almost all black and almost all stare back at the white man in his Cadillac.

A group of young men stare threateningly as he rolls past.

On the street, in the lee of a Brownstone staircase, a deal is going down.

A172 ROBERT AND SETH ABRAHMS - DAY   A172

sit in a coffee shop.

> SETH
> (genuinely surprised)
> She's not at that place you sent her?

> ROBERT
> She snuck away. And we haven't seen her.
> She hasn't come home.

> SETH
> Oh, man --

> ROBERT
> She hasn't called you?

> SETH
> I tried to talk to her when she was up
> there, but they wouldn't put me through.
> (beat)
> I'm surprised she hasn't called.

172   ANOTHER ANGLE ON ROBERT IN THE CAR - DAY   172

He turns a corner and is suddenly in a drive-thru drug market. Dealers, HUSTLERS, run at the windows from both sides, signalling.

172 CONTINUED: 172

                    HUSTLERS
          What you want? Rock? Rock? Hey, what you
          want?

A173 ROBERT AND SETH - DAY   A173

     in the coffee shop.

                    ROBERT
          Can you tell me anything? Do you have any
          ideas?

                    SETH
          I don't know what to say.

                    ROBERT
          I'm not the police. I don't care about
          experimentation. She's a kid. I'm worried
          to death.

                    SETH
          You won't say anything to my parents?

                    ROBERT
          I don't give a fuck about your parents --

                    SETH
          We sometimes went downtown to score.

                    ROBERT
          What?

                    SETH
          The West End. We buy it off the streets.
              (beat)
          I can stop, you know, and she can't. Two
          people, really similar, we can talk about
          anything, but for me it's like a weekend
          thing, then I get my shit together, and
          for her it's different --

                    ROBERT
          You don't know what the hell you're
          talking about. You're a cocky seventeen
          year-old and you don't have a clue what
          the stakes are. You don't know the value
          of the life you've yet to throw away. And
          neither does she.

173 ROBERT IN HIS CAR - DAY   173

     It is surrounded. Robert stares. A face presses up against
     the window.

                                              (CONTINUED)

                         FACE
                  (through the window)
            What do you want?

                         ROBERT
                  (through the window)
            What do you mean, what do I want?

                         FACE
            Rock or dope, man?

                         ROBERT
            I don't want anything.

174   ROBERT AND SETH   174

                         SETH
            Hey man, I'm sorry. I'm just trying to
            help.

                         ROBERT
            You want to help? Stay the fuck away from
            her.

A175 ROBERT IN HIS CAR   A175

                    ROBERT (cont'd)
            I'm looking for my daughter.

The dealer looks at him with disgust, turns his back, and
waves everyone else away.

Robert slams his fist against the steering wheel. He slams it
again and again. He stops and pulls away, just as

AT THE INTERSECTION

behind Robert's car, Caroline crosses the street toward
Sketch's house.

175   INT. SKETCH'S BEDROOM - DAY   175

A single candle lights the room. Caroline is underneath
Sketch the drug dealer. He is pounding away. As she clutches
his back and holds on, her expression is both surprised and
druggy, and SOUNDS escape her mouth that she wouldn't believe
she could make.

There's a KNOCK on the door. Sketch continues his business.
The KNOCKING is more insistent. Finally, he stops and gets up
and goes to the door. Caroline lies back. She's in a bed with
black sheets in a room with nothing else in it but a dresser
and some duffle bags.

                                              (CONTINUED)

Sketch opens the door --

                    SKETCH
          What the fuck do you want?

SOMEBODY outside says something. Sketch walks over to a
duffle bag and extracts some product. Caroline's eyes are
glued to it as Sketch hands it through the door. Sketch sees
her staring at the drugs.

He comes back to bed.

                    SKETCH (CONT'D)
          You want some of that?

Caroline nods.

                    SKETCH (cont'd)
          What you gonna do to get some of that?

                    CAROLINE
          Please --

                    SKETCH
          What you gonna do?

She turns her back to him, pouting. He laughs.

                    SKETCH (CONT'D)
          Maybe a taste.

He reaches over beside the bed where there is a small tray.
On the tray is a rig, spoon, several powders, and an eye
dropper. He pulls the candle over and rapidly fixes a
speedball. He pulls the fluid into the neck of the syringe
and holds it up the light. It has Caroline transfixed.

                    SKETCH (cont'd)
          Feed this to you like a little bird.

He squirts the tiniest amount of fluid into the air. It arcs
in the candlelight.

                    CAROLINE
          Don't --

                    SKETCH
          You want this?

She nods.

                                        (CONTINUED)

>   SKETCH (cont'd)
>   This is the Express train. Baby turnin'
>   pro and getting down in a big, big hole.

Her concentration is entirely, hypnotically focused on the
syringe.

Sketch moves the syringe toward her lips.

>   SKETCH (cont'd)
>   Kiss it. Kiss your new mommy hello.

Caroline moves her mouth toward the side of the syringe, her
lips part.

Sketch pulls the sheet back, exposing her legs. He grips one
powerful hand around her ankle and squeezes... Veins stand
out on her foot.

He slides the needle into the largest vein and slowly
depresses the plunger.

Caroline watches, then her head tilts back, then forward, she
GROANS sexually and slumps against the pillows, her eyes half-
open, her lips twitching.

Sketch puts the rig back on the tray, then admires Caroline's
beauty for a second before starting to fuck her again.

                                                          CUT TO:

176   EXT. HOTEL - DAY   176

Gordon and Castro and two other AGENTS escort Ruiz out of the
hotel and usher him into a waiting cruiser.

They pull out in a caravan and move through the streets
toward the courthouse.

177   EXT. COURTHOUSE PARKING LOT - DAY   177

The cruiser pulls into a fenced and gated parking lot.

Gordon, Castro and Ruiz, walking with a limp, cross to the
building entrance.

As they push inside, Francisco Flores, in a conservative grey
suit passes them going outside.

The parking lot is empty of people. The guards at the gate
talk about something distracting.

                                                      (CONTINUED)

177 CONTINUED: 177

Francisco passes by the cruiser and drops his keys. Kneeling
down he extracts a small, powerful, magnetized bomb from his
jacket. He attaches it to the underside of the vehicle,
stands and walks toward the guard gate.

178 INT. COURTROOM - DAY   178

The court is filled to capacity. Helena and Metzger watch
from the gallery.

The JUDGE bangs his gavel. Adler is on his feet.

                    ADLER
          Your honor, it has come to our attention
          that your honor, while in private
          practice, previously represented the town
          of Seal Beach in their stop-work suit
          against the Police Department of Seal
          Beach. We believe this disqualifies you
          from hearing this case and we therefore
          move for a temporary suspension while
          this is investigated.

The judge is surprised to hear this.

                    JUDGE
          Mr. Adler, this is a most unusual motion.

                    ADLER
          Nonetheless, your honor, we feel that our
          client deserves every fairness afforded
          under the law.

                    JUDGE
          If this is in any way designed to delay
          the testimony of Eduardo Ruiz...

The judge considers.

                    JUDGE (CONT'D)
          We'll recess until 9:00 am Monday
          morning. And I'll see counsel in
          chambers.

He slams the gavel down again.

179 EXT. COURTHOUSE - DAY   179

Gordon, Castro, other AGENTS and Ruiz come down the rear
steps of the courthouse and walk across the street toward the
parking lot.

                                                    (CONTINUED)

179   CONTINUED: 179

                         CASTRO
              Remember when we sat on that mob guy,
              that chef, for like six months?

                         GORDON
              Oh, man, I've never eaten so good in my
              life.
                   (to Ruiz)
              Why don't you develop a useful skill?

                         CASTRO
              Yeah, like turning into a beautiful
              woman.

They reach the car.

                         RUIZ
              Would you mind if today we walked? It's
              one block. I could use the fresh air.

180   OMITTED   180

181   INT. FRANCISCO'S CAR - CONTINUOUS   181

Across the street, Francisco, encrypted cell phone to his
ear, watches from his own car as Gordon, Castro, and Ruiz
stand by their car without getting in, then walk away from
the car.

                         FRANCISCO
                   (into phone)
              They're not getting into the car. What
              are they doing? They're walking right at
              me.

The men start across the street toward Francisco.

182   INT. HELENA'S CAR - DAY   182

Helena drives her car through downtown San Diego.

                         HELENA
                   (into phone)
              You've got a gun. Get out of the car and
              shoot him in the head.

183   INT. FRANCISCO'S CAR - DAY   183

Francisco watches Ruiz and the agents walk up the street
toward him.

                                                        (CONTINUED)

183   CONTINUED: 183

                          FRANCISCO
                       (into phone)
                They're going to walk right past me.

                          HELENA (V.O.)
                What are you? A mouse? Get out of the car
                and do it. This is your chance.

Francisco watches the three men walk past his car. He makes a
decision and opens his door.

184   EXT. STREET - DAY   184

Francisco steps from the car and mingles in with OTHER PEOPLE
walking along the sidewalk. He follows them for few yards,
picking his moment.

He closes the distance to Gordon, Castro and Ruiz, pulling a
pistol from inside his jacket. He takes careful aim from
twelve feet away and is about to shoot Ruiz when a bullet
hole appears in his chest. He staggers, trying to squeeze the
trigger,

Francisco fires the gun once, wildly --

A TOURIST SCREAMS --

Gordon and Castro and Ruiz turn --

Francisco is looking down at the widening red splotch in the
center of his shirt, uncertain of what has happened --

Gordon shoves Ruiz down into a doorway and fires three quick
shots --

Francisco spins around and drops on his face in the street.

Citizens run in all directions fearing a psychopath with an
NRA card coming off a bad week of day-trading --

Gordon and Castro with Ruiz beneath them scan the streets.

                          CASTRO
                Stay here. I'll get the car.

Castro runs down the street for the court parking lot. Other
AGENTS are running toward Gordon and Ruiz.

185   INT. OFFICE BUILDING WINDOW - CONTINUOUS   185

The STRANGE MAN who threatened Helena's children packs a high-
caliber rifle and scope into a briefcase.

                                                        (CONTINUED)

185   CONTINUED: 185

He snaps the case shut and quickly exits the room. We notice
a man on the floor with a bullet hole in his head next to the
open door.

186   EXT. STREET - CONTINUOUS   186

Agents surround Ruiz.

Gordon walks to the body of Francisco lying face down in the
gutter. He turns him over with his shoe and sees his face.

                     GORDON
                (to the other agents)
            I saw this guy at the courthouse.
                (beat)
            The car --

Gordon takes off running, yelling for Castro.

187   EXT. COURT PARKING LOT - DAY   187

Castro has reached the car and gets in.

Gordon appears at the gate of the lot --

                     GORDON
                   (yelling)
            No --

188   INT. CRUISER - DAY   188

Castro turns the ignition exactly at the moment he sees
Gordon yelling and waving his arms --

189   EXT. COURT PARKING LOT - DAY   189

The cruiser EXPLODES.

Gordon hits the pavement. Parts of the car begin raining down
around him.

                                                        CUT TO:

190   OMITTED   190

A191   INT. SIDEWALK CAFE - SAN DIEGO - DAY   A191

A fire truck and paramedic unit WHIZZES by. Manolo sits at an
outdoor cafe table, waiting. He can't help looking around at
the attractive people, but he's also nervous.

                                                      (CONTINUED)

A191 CONTINUED: A191

Suddenly two MEN, recognizable as Salazar's OFFICERS from the
desert drug bust, sitting at a nearby table, rise and move to
Manolo's table.

                         MAN #1
                 Manolo, how are you?

They take seats uncomfortably close to Manolo.

                         MAN #2
                 Manolo, have we interrupted? You're
                 looking around like you're expecting
                 someone.

                         MANOLO
                 No. I'm looking for the waiter. I want to
                 order.

                         MAN #1
                 What are you gonna have?

                         MANOLO
                 A steak.

                         MAN #1
                 Well, if you like steak, we know a much
                 better place. We'll take you there.

                         MANOLO
                 That's okay, really.

They each take Manolo by an arm.

                         MAN #2
                 Manolo, we should really be going now,
                 before it gets too crowded.

B191 INT. SUV - DAY   B191

We're looking through the windshield as we approach the
Mexican border. As the car slows, we pan to follow the border
official as he looks in briefly and waves us through. We
continue the pan to reveal Manolo in the backseat sitting
beside Man #2.

C191 INT. SUV - DAY   C191

We're in the desert. There's nothing in any direction. Javi
is implacable. Manolo understands what is happening.

                                                    (CONTINUED)

  C191

                    MANOLO
          I was going to feed them wrong
          information. Feed them lies to ... it was
          for...

The men say nothing. After a beat --

                    MANOLO (CONT'D)
          Don't tell Anna I died like this. Tell
          her it was something else. Tell her it
          was official business. Tell her that I
          died doing something honorable. Please,
          tell her that for me...

EXT. DESERT - DAY

Javi and Manolo stand next to two freshly dug graves.

                    MAN #1
          Turn around.

Javi hesitates before turning. We're on Javi as we hear the
GUNSHOT. Javi doesn't flinch. Manolo's body falls into the
grave.

Javi stands there, waiting.

                    MAN #1 (CONT'D)
          You got anything you want to say?

Javi shakes his head. Finally, another GUNSHOT. After a beat,
a hand reaches out of Javi's shoulder.

                    MAN #1 (CONT'D)
          Sorry about that... we had to be sure.

They walk back to the SUV.

                    SOMEBODY ELSE
          Are you sure you don't have anything to
          tell us?

Javi says nothing, doesn't even acknowledge them. We hear a
GUNSHOT.

                                                      CUT TO:

191   INT. AYALA HOME - DAY   191

Arnie Metzger is in Helena's living room. The stereo is
loudly playing MOZART.

                                                  (CONTINUED)

                         ARNIE
             That was a stupid thing you did.
             Incredibly stupid.

                         HELENA
             I tried, Arnie. And, I will continue to
             try.

                         ARNIE
             Have you gone crazy? You are not Carl.
             You aren't as good as Carl.
                  (beat)
             They are moving the trial to a high
             security location. The press has gone
             berserk. The jury will be influenced.
             Stay out of things. Let us try to win the
             case.

                         HELENA
             That is going to be rather difficult when
             all the evidence is against us.

Helena steps closer to Arnie, close enough that her breasts
are almost touching his chest.

                         ARNIE
             Helena, please. This is out of your
             hands.

                         HELENA
                  (softly)
             I know I made things worse. I know that
             and I'm sorry, but Arnie I need something
             from you. Something only you can help me
             with.

Helena looks searchingly into his eyes.

                         ARNIE
             Helena --

                         HELENA
             I need an introduction to the Obregon
             Brothers.

                         ARNIE
             I can't do that.

Helena leans closer to him.

191   CONTINUED: (2)   191

                         HELENA
              I've figured out what Carl was up to and
              I need your help. Will you help me?

                                                      CUT TO:

192   EXT. LABORATORY RESEARCH FACILITIES - DAY   192

       An establishing shot of a hi-tech company within shooting
       distance of the Salk Institute.

193   INT. LAB FACILITY - DAY   193

       This is a professional chemical lab that can be rented by the
       month. Long tables of lab and computer equipment. Nobody has
       been here in a while. There are toys - plastic dolls,
       frisbees, hula hoops - on many of the tables.

       Helena lets herself into the room. She scans ledgers. She
       looks over the equipment.

       She picks up a twelve-inch high plastic Spastic Jack action
       figure and a can labeled "solvent" and hurries from the lab.

                                                      CUT TO:

194   EXT. WEST END - CINCINNATI - NIGHT   194

       Robert drives through the streets, searching for Caroline. He
       doesn't find her.

195   INT. WAKEFIELD HOUSE - NIGHT   195

       Barbara is waiting in the living room. Robert enters. He
       shakes his head then stands silently for a beat.

                         ROBERT
              About the other night, I'm sorry.

                         BARBARA
              Me, too.

                         ROBERT
              God, I don't get it. Are we supposed to
              say to ourselves, be prepared to lose
              her, be prepared to lose our child?
                    (beat)
              Why does this happen to someone? How does
              it happen?

                         BARBARA
              I don't know.

196   INT. CAROLINE'S BEDROOM - NIGHT   196

    Robert is standing in the middle of her room. He's not sure
    what he's looking for. Everywhere he looks: her personal
    things, beloved objects from more innocent times, pictures.

    Within moments a legitimate desire to connect with his
    daughter has escalated into a search for clues. He opens her
    drawers, dumps little boxes, pulls things off of shelves.

    He becomes increasingly unhinged, flinging things around her
    room. He tosses a stack of magazines. A fashion magazine,
    airborne, discharges some contents: a lighter, a plastic tube
    and a piece of folded aluminum foil fluttering to the ground.

    Robert stares at the foil on the carpet. It's charred on the
    outside. He picks it up. And unfolds it. There's a dried
    milky white substance.

    He picks up the tube and lighter and stares at them. Then,
    somewhat tentatively, he puts the tube in his mouth. He holds
    the lighter under the foil, then heats the milky substance
    which turns translucent and disappears in a cloud of smoke.
    Robert sucks all of it in.

    He waits a long time then exhales. His eyes shut. The tube
    drops from his mouth. He staggers and, overwhelmed by the
    sensations, sits on the bed. The lighter and foil fall from
    his hand.

    A moment later he opens his eyes and doesn't seem to know
    where he is. He looks at the room, confused. He stumbles to
    the door and shuts it firmly behind him.

                                                   CUT TO:

A197   INT. MANOLO'S HOUSE - DAY   A197

    Anna is weeping. Javier sits next to her. He puts his arm
    around her and she leans her head against his shoulder.

B197   INT. JAVIER'S SUV - DAY   B197

    Javi drives through the streets of Tijuana. He brakes for a
    stop sign and watches, trance-like, the pedestrians crossing
    in front of him. As the intersection clears he remains still.

    A HONK from behind brings him back and he pulls forward
    passing Helena Ayala who crosses going the opposite
    direction. We stay with her.

                                                   CUT TO:

197   EXT. TIJUANA - DAY   197

Helena walks down a nightlife street that is tawdry and stale
in the midday sun.

198   OMITTED   198

199   INT. CLUB PLATINUM - DAY   199

A shrewd Obregon Lieutenant, JUAN MARQUEZ, 40, sits at a
table opposite Helena. The Strange Man who both threatened
Helena's child and executed Francisco sits in another chair.

                    MARQUEZ
          Mrs. Ayala. Thank you for coming. I am
          Juan Marquez, I work for Mr. Obregon. I
          believe you know my associate,
          "Tigrillo," the Little Tiger.

Helena nods to Tigrillo --

                    HELENA
          Yes, he threatened to kill my five year-
          old son.
                    (beat)
          I was under the impression I would be
          meeting Juan Obregon.

                    MARQUEZ
          No, that is not possible. And thank you
          for coming down here, though I suspect
          it's been a pointless journey.

                    HELENA
          Why do you say that, Mr. Marquez?

                    MARQUEZ
          I hear these stories. Your husband in
          jail. His business in chaos. Various
          people fighting over the scraps.

                    HELENA
          My husband is the victim of an informer
          in your organization, not ours.

                    MARQUEZ
          That is not true, Mrs. Ayala. Your route
          is compromised. Perhaps it is time for me
          to deal with other distributors in
          California.

                    HELENA
          I don't think you're going to do that.

                                        (CONTINUED)

> MARQUEZ
> You don't? Listen to this woman in a
> man's world, a very violent world.

> HELENA
> There are plenty of other suppliers in
> Mexico.

> MARQUEZ
> But not in whose interest it is to help
> you out of debt.

Helena reaches into her bag and pulls out the Spastic Jack
action figure. She puts it on the desk.

> HELENA
> My husband had been working on something
> he called, *The Project for the Children*.
> Are you aware of this?

> MARQUEZ
> I don't know. Perhaps I remember
> something.

> HELENA
> We have the ability to change the color,
> odor, and physical property of cocaine.

> MARQUEZ
> You want to smuggle narcotics in Mr.
> Espastico Jacobo. That's nothing new.

> HELENA
> Not in...

Juan Marquez is confused.

> HELENA (cont'd)
> This doll *is* cocaine.

Juan picks up Spastic Jack and looks at him. He bangs it on
the desk.

> HELENA (cont'd)
> Every part, from his ears to his
> accessory belt, is high-impact, pressure-
> molded cocaine. Odorless. Undetectable by
> dogs. Undetectable by anyone.

> MARQUEZ
> I don't believe you.

She takes out the "solvent" and puts it on his desk.

(CONTINUED)

                            HELENA
                    Get a bowl.

200   INT. CLUB PLATINUM - OFFICE - LATER   200

      Spastic Jack is slowly dissolving in a bowl of solvent. Only
      his shoulders, head, and ridiculous ears remain above the
      quicksand of milky glop.

      Helena holds a mirror under the desk lamp. She is drying the
      paste. She puts the mirror on the desk. A white substance has
      coagulated there.

                            HELENA
                    Try it.

      Juan takes out a razor blade and chops the dried substance
      into two white powder lines. He hands a silver straw to
      Helena.

                            MARQUEZ
                    You first.

                            HELENA
                    I'm six months pregnant. I won't do it.

                            MARQUEZ
                    Fine, then we don't have deal.

                            HELENA
                    Fine, then we don't have a deal.

      She stands. He watches her a beat, then smiles.

                            MARQUEZ
                    Okay, okay.

      He leans down and quickly snorts a line. After a beat.

                            Marquez (cont'd)
                    That's good coke.

                            HELENA
                    It should be... It's yours.
                        (beat)
                    I want our debt forgiven. I want to be
                    the exclusive distributor of Obregon
                    Brothers Cocaine for the United States.
                    And I want the principle witness against
                    my husband, Eduardo Ruiz, killed.

200   CONTINUED: 200

                         MARQUEZ
              Perhaps... Perhaps... I'm afraid I must
              first ask you to pass a test. I asked the
              same of your husband and he succeeded
              with flying colors.

Helena waits. Juan Marquez reaches in his desk and pulls out
a quarter kilo of cocaine. He pushes it across the desk.

                         MARQUEZ (cont'd)
              Take this back with you. Deliver it
              safely to Tigrillo in San Diego and we
              have a deal.

                         HELENA
              That's crazy. My husband is on trial for
              smuggling.

                         MARQUEZ
              Exactly, and this is how I know I'm not
              getting into business with the U.S.
              Government.

She puts the quarter key in her bag and stands.

                         HELENA
              You will help me with my other problem.

                         MARQUEZ
              Deliver that safely to Tigrillo in San
              Diego. And we have a deal.

Tigrillo escorts her out of the room.

201   INT. CLUB PLATINUM - DAY   201

Helena follows Tigrillo. As they pass the restrooms she
signals that she has to stop.

202   INT. CLUB PLATINUM - LADIES' ROOM - DAY   202

Helena goes into a stall. She extracts the cocaine from her
handbag.

She looks at it, trying to figure out where it goes. She
hikes up her skirt.

                                                    CUT TO:

203   OMITTED   203

204   OMITTED   204

205   OMITTED   205

206   OMITTED   206

207   OMITTED   207

208   OMITTED   208

209   OMITTED   209

210   INT. HOTEL ROOM - DAY   210

Javier is hooked up to a polygraph machine watched closely by
a POLYGRAPH OPERATOR. Hughes and Johnson watch as Javi talks
into a tape recorder on the table.

                    JAVIER
          ... And I have the electronic serial
          numbers for their cellular phones. They
          change them every twenty-four hours but I
          have a contact at MexTel who can get me
          the new ESNs within twelve.

Javi finishes talking and sits back. Agent Hughes shuts off
the tape recorder and looks at the polygraph operator who
nods approval. Hughes and Johnson exchange a look. They are
dumbstruck.

                    HUGHES
          That's good shit.

                    JAVIER
          Now that you have what you want, let's
          talk about how I get what I want.

                    JOHNSON
          Oh, don't worry, Javier, you're not gonna
          have any problems there.

                    HUGHES
          I want to take a minute and talk about
          what type of precautions you're taking to
          protect yourself. When Salazar and
          Madrigal go down, they might send someone
          to see you.

                    JAVIER
          You worry about getting me the things
          that I want. I'll worry about myself.

There's a beat. Javier seems discomfited. The two agents
notice this and exchange looks.

                                          (CONTINUED)

210   CONTINUED: 210

                              JOHNSON
                    You should feel good about this.

                              JAVIER
                    I feel like a traitor.

                                                          CUT TO:

211   OMITTED   211

212   OMITTED   212

213   EXT. BORDER CROSSING AUTOMOBILE CHECKPOINT - DAY   213

      Javi goes into Mexico. Pan over to Helena's Mercedes.

214   INT. HELENA'S CAR - DAY   214

      She inches the car forward towards the officer who selects
      vehicles for inspection. The car ahead of her passes through
      and speeds away. The OFFICER flags Helena and directs her
      into the search facility.

215   EXT. CUSTOMS SEARCH BAY - DAY   215

      Helena pulls into a search bay.

      A CUSTOMS OFFICER watches Helena lower her window.

                         CUSTOMS OFFICER
                    Please step from the car, Ma'am.

                              HELENA
                    I'm in a hurry --

                         CUSTOMS OFFICER
                    Step from the car, Ma'am. This won't take
                    long from your day.

      Helena gets out of her car.

216   INT. OBSERVATION ROOM - CUSTOMS CHECKPOINT - DAY   216

      There is a bank of video monitors showing the scenes all over
      the facility.

      ON THE MONITOR: Helena's car is on a lift three feet off the
      ground. Officers pour over the inside and undercarriage of
      the Mercedes.

      Nearby, A GERMAN SHEPHERD sniffs at the items that have been
      removed from the car: bags, spare tire, cd boxes.

217   EXT. CUSTOMS SEARCH BAY - DAY   217

Customs OFFICERS approach Helena --

                    OFFICER
          Ma'am, we have to ask you to come with
          us.

She follows them toward the Customs building.

218   INT. STRIP SEARCH ROOM - DAY   218

A FEMALE CUSTOMS INSPECTOR accompanied by a female
SUPERVISORY INSPECTOR leads Helena into a sterile room where
there is no place to hide anything.

                    CUSTOMS MATRON
          Ma'am, we have reason to believe you may
          have illegal drugs hidden beneath your
          clothing. I need to conduct a pat down
          search. Supervisory Inspector Haig will
          witness the search.

                    HELENA
          You've got to be kidding me. I'm
          pregnant. What if I refuse?

                    CUSTOMS MATRON
          This pamphlet explains the law and your
          rights under it. You're welcome to read
          it first. It says we have the authority
          to conduct this search. Would you like to
          read it first or shall we proceed?

A219 EXT. FUNERAL SERVICE - DAY   A219

Hundreds of DEA AGENTS, spouses, others stand around a grave
in a leafy cemetery in working class San Diego.

B219 EXT. CEMETERY - DAY   B219

The funeral is over and people are filing back to the cars.
Gordon walks away from the service when he is approached by a
mourning LUCINDA CASTRO, the mother of the deceased.

                    MRS. CASTRO
          Montel... Oh, Montel.

Gordon hugs her.

                    MRS. CASTRO (cont'd)
          You know how much he cared about you. You
          do, don't you?

(CONTINUED)

> GORDON
> Yes.

> MRS. CASTRO
> I know if he could have it back somehow,
> he wouldn't do it differently or have it
> any other way. He wouldn't. He loved his
> job.

Another AGENT hustles toward him from the other direction,
the direction of the cars.

> AGENT
> Excuse me, Agent Gordon. Mrs. Castro.
>   (to Gordon)
> Helena Ayala left Club Platinum in
> Tijuana. The Obregon Brothers' place.
> They stopped her at the border but she
> was clean. She's in San Diego now.

Gordon runs for his car.

> CUT TO:

219   INT. ARNIE METZGER'S OFFICE - DAY   219

Arnie sits in his office, spacing out, admiring his view when
an ASSISTANT shows Helena in. As soon as the door shuts --

> HELENA
> Did you get it?

> ARNIE
> What are you thinking, calling me at home
> with a message like that? You've
> compromised me and our relationship --

Helena sits confidently on his couch.

> HELENA
>   (making fun of Arnie)
> The place is swept twice a day. I learned
> that down in Miami in '85...
>   (hard)
> Arnie. I'm the housewife. I belong to the
> most exclusive country club in La Jolla
> that accepts Latinos. Until recently, I
> believed my husband imported hydroponic
> strawberries, which I donated at the
> school fair.

Arnie reaches into a desk drawer and pulls out a quarter-kilo
baggy identical to the one Juan Obregon gave her in Tijuana.

> (CONTINUED)

219   CONTINUED: 219

                              HELENA (CONT'D)
                    It's the same stuff? From the rainy day
                    stash?

                              ARNIE
                    It's the same. What happened to what they
                    gave you?

Helena puts the bag in her purse.

                              HELENA
                    I'm desperate, but I'm not stupid. I
                    flushed it in the bathroom of their
                    godawful nightclub.

                                                        CUT TO:

220   OMITTED   220

A221   INT. ROBERT AND BARBARA'S BEDROOM - EARLY MORNING   A221

Robert sleeps in his clothes on top of the covers. Barbara is
asleep beside him. The phone rings. Robert answers. Barbara
watches.

                              ROBERT
                    Hello.

                              SHERIDAN (V.O.)
                    I'm sorry... Did I wake you?

Robert looks at Barbara and shakes his head. She gets up.

                              ROBERT
                    No, it's all right.

There's a beat.

                              SHERIDAN (V.O.)
                    Salazar's been taken down. He was working
                    for Porfirio Madrigal.

                              ROBERT
                    What? I thought Madrigal was dead. I
                    thought it was verified.

                              SHERIDAN (V.O.)
                    Apparently not. Look, it's a shit storm
                    here right now. When are you coming back?
                        (beat)
                    I don't know what to tell people any
                    more.

                                                        (CONTINUED)

                    ROBERT
          I'll get there as soon as I can.

                    SHERIDAN (V.O.)
          If we're moving the press conference, we
          need to do it now.
               (beat)
          Are you all right?

                    BARBARA WAKEFIELD (V.O.)
          Robert.

The tone in Barbara's voice causes him to look up. She holds
an empty jewelry box.

                    ROBERT
               (to Sheridan)
          I have to call you back.

B221 INT. DINING ROOM - EARLY MORNING   B221

The drawers and cabinets are open. Barbara and Robert assess
what is missing.

                    BARBARA
          The silver wedding cup.

C221 INT. LIVING ROOM - EARLY MORNING   C221

Robert looks at their home entertainment center. Barbara
enters this room.

                    BARBARA
          My Leica's gone.

                    ROBERT
          So's the video camera.

                    BARBARA
          At least she's alive.

Robert turns for the door.

                    BARBARA (cont'd)
          Where are you going?

                    ROBERT
          She'll be at a pawn shop in an hour. Ten
          minutes after that she'll be at her
          dealer's. If I find him, maybe I find
          her.

D221 INT. CLASSROOM - CINCINNATI COUNTRY DAY - DAY   D221

The bored children of privilege, wearing their blazers or
uniform grey skirts, stare at a TEACHER behind a desk.

The door opens and Robert enters. He finds Seth Abrahms in
the back of the class and walks straight to him. Robert grabs
a fistful of shirt and tie.

                    SETH
          Hey man, what are you doing?

                    TEACHER (O.S.)
          Excuse me? Excuse me?

Robert yanks Seth out of his seat. The teacher is
approaching.

                    ROBERT
          Seth has to be excused. He's going on a
          field trip.

221   INT. THE FUN ZONE - DAY   221

Helena watches David play a video game. They have finished
their lunch, a mess of pizza rinds.

                    HELENA
          Come on. Time to go.

The CLOWN tries to catch their attention with some mime, but
they ignore him.

222   EXT. THE FUN ZONE - DAY   222

Helena and David are pushing out the door. The man walking
the other way past them is Tigrillo from the Tijuana cartel.
As they pass --

                    HELENA
               (under her breath)
          Women's room, stall two.
               (loud)
          Should we stop for ice-cream?

                    DAVID
          Yeah!

Tigrillo disappears into the restaurant.

(CONTINUED)

222   CONTINUED: 222

       As Helena pulls out of the Fun Zone parking lot, an unmarked
       DEA cruiser falls in behind her.

                                                            CUT TO:

A223   INT. ROBERT'S CAR - DAY   A223

       Robert and Seth are parked across the street from Sketch's
       building. They watch people, mostly white people, get what
       they need.

                         SETH
              I don't know, maybe we missed her.

                         ROBERT
              I can't believe you used to bring my
              daughter here, to this place.

                         SETH
              Hey man, back the fuck up. *To this place.*
              What's that shit? Right now, all over
              this country, a hundred thousand white
              people from the suburbs are driving
              around downtown asking every black person
              they see, *You got any drugs? You know
              where I can get drugs?* What kind of
              effect you think this has on the psyche
              of a black person, on their
              possibilities? If you sent a hundred
              thousand black people into *your*
              neighborhood, Indian Hills, and they
              asked every white person they saw, *hey,
              you got any drugs?*, within a day, your
              friends and their kids would be selling.
              It's market forces, man. The product's
              marked up three hundred percent. You can
              go out on the street and make five
              hundred bucks in two hours and then do
              whatever you want for the rest of the
              day. You think white people would still
              be going to law school?

       There's a beat.

                         ROBERT
              You're starting to piss me off. Get out
              of the car.

       Robert and Seth get out of the car and walk across the
       street.

B223 INT. HALLWAY - DAY   B223

Robert and Seth stand in the dim, dingy hallway. A JUNKIE
leaves.

                    SETH
          You're gonna get me killed.

Robert shoves Seth toward the door. Seth knocks. The door
opens a crack and Sketch's face appears.

                    SKETCH
          What do you want?

Robert moves around Seth.

                    ROBERT
          I'm looking for my daughter, Caroline.
          She comes here.

                    SKETCH
          This is a business. Get the fuck outta
          here.

                    ROBERT
          I need to find my daughter. I'll pay you.

Sketch pulls a gun and shoves it against Robert's cheek.

                    SKETCH
          Who the fuck do you think you are? Where
          the fuck do you think you are? Why the
          fuck do you think I shouldn't just put
          you in a dumpster?

                    ROBERT
          I have money --

                    SKETCH
          I got money.

                    ROBERT
          I'll pay you a thousand dollars. I have
          it in my wallet.

                    SKETCH
          I want your money, I'll take your money.

                    ROBERT
          Just tell me where she is.

                                              (CONTINUED)

B223 CONTINUED: B223

Sketch pushes Robert back into the hall. Sketch sees Seth
lurking there.

                    SKETCH
                 (to Seth)
            Don't do that shit again.

Sketch slams the door in their face.

                    SETH
            Great. What a good idea.

C223 EXT. STREET - DAY   C223

Seth and Robert walk to the car.

                    SETH
            Man, I'm telling you. Don't do this
            vigilante thing. Either the cops find her
            or she'll call you. I promise.

Robert looks at him, carefully.

                                                      CUT TO:

D223 EXT. MANOLO'S HOUSE - DAY   D223

Javier KNOCKS on the front door. There is no answer. The
shades are drawn. The house is darkened.

                    JAVIER
                 (calling out)
            Anna. Anna, please. Let me in.

He KNOCKS again.

                    JAVIER (cont'd)
            Come on. You can't stay locked in your
            house all day.

Finally, the door cracks open. Anna has clearly not been out
of the house since the last time we saw her.

E223 INT. MANOLO'S HOUSE - DAY   E223

Javier sits opposite Anna.

                    JAVIER
            I know this is a tragedy, but you have to
            realize that good has come out of it.

She looks at him.

                                                      (CONTINUED)

>   JAVIER (cont'd)
>   If Manolo hadn't gone and told them what
>   he did then Salazar and Madrigal would
>   never have been brought to justice. He
>   did a great thing for Tijuana. He did a
>   great thing for Mexico.

>   ANNA
>   I want to believe you. I really do.

>   JAVIER
>   You will believe me, because it's true.

223   EXT. SKETCH'S APARTMENT - DAY   223

Seth walks up the steps and into the building. A beat later
he reappears and continues down the street.

Robert emerges from across the street and follows at a
guarded distance.

224   EXT. STREETS - DAY   224

Seth walks along the seedy neighborhood street. He approaches
the Villa Elaine. He turns up the steps and disappears
inside.

Robert follows him.

225   INT. VILLA ELAINE HALLWAY - DAY   225

Robert ascends the stairs. As he enters the hallway he sees
Seth pounding on one of the doors.

>   SETH
>   Open the door. Open the fucking door,
>   man.

A MAN'S VOICE comes from the other side of the door.

>   MUFFLED VOICE
>   Go away!

Robert closes the distance. Seth pounds harder.

>   SETH
>   I know she's in there. Let me talk to
>   her.

>   MUFFLED VOICE
>   I don't know what you're talking about.
>   Go away!

                                                       (CONTINUED)

225   CONTINUED: 225

Robert reaches the door. Seth sees him.

                        SETH
            I know she's in there.

Robert kicks the door in.

226   INT. HOTEL ROOM - DAY   226

Robert sees a middle-aged JOHN in his underwear and a dress
shirt.

                        JOHN
            Hey, I haven't touched her --

Caroline is passed out on the bed. Robert goes to her as the
John scrambles for his clothes.

She stirs and sees him --

                        CAROLINE
                    (really out of it)
            Hi, Daddy.

227   INT. ROBERT'S CAR - DAY   227

Caroline rides in the passenger seat. She's come out of her
stupor and is now filled with ebullience.

                        CAROLINE
            It's gonna be great... I mean, I'm okay
            and all, because, see, I met a guy, he's
            in this pretty famous band and...
                    (gets up confessional courage)
            They've invited me to write lyrics for
            them, I'm gonna be able to do that and
            maybe sing, too... not at first, but
            later.

Caroline gets lost in her grandiose vision. Robert looks over
at her as she drifts off into a nod. A moment later she's
awake and rambling again.

                        CAROLINE (cont'd)
                    (sounding completely crazy)
            I've been doing research for the school
            paper, that's what I've been doing, like
            on assignment kind-of, I've seen some
            stuff you wouldn't believe, but I'm gonna
            write it all down into lyrics. They think
            I'm really good, everybody says so, what
            do you think?

                                                    (CONTINUED)

227   CONTINUED: 227

Robert fights back tears. He reaches over and takes his
daughter's hand.

                                                            CUT TO:

228   OMITTED   228

229   OMITTED   229

230   OMITTED   230

231   OMITTED   231

232   OMITTED   232

233   OMITTED   233

234   OMITTED   234

235   OMITTED   235

A236 INT. CLUB PLATINUM OFFICE - DAY   A236

Juan Marquez sits across the desk from Javi. Tigrillo and
PABLO, 30's, are also in the meeting.

                    MARQUEZ
          Salazar and Madrigal are no longer with
          us.
               (beat)
          A feat none of these people could get
          accomplished.

Juan nods toward Pablo and Tigrillo.

                    MARQUEZ (cont'd)
          You're going to be made the Special
          Assistant to the new drug Czar, which
          makes you a very valuable law enforcement
          officer.
               (beat)
          I hope you like to travel because we have
          plans for Juarez and El Paso, Nogales,
          Sinaloa, Jalisco, Michoacan...

Javi just stares at him for a long moment, then looks off.

                                                            CUT TO:

236   INT. ROBERT'S OFFICE IN WASHINGTON - DAY   236

Robert on the telephone.

                         ROBERT
                     (into phone)
                 How was she?

237   INT. BARBARA'S OFFICE - DAY   237

A cramped, messy office at the Environmental Protection
Agency. Barbara is on the phone.

                         BARBARA
                     (into phone)
                 I'm really not sure. She seemed to
                 recognize it wasn't Serenity Oaks. It's a
                 pretty hard-core facility, but at least
                 we know where she is.
                     (beat)
                 Maybe it's what she needs now.

A238   INTERCUT ROBERT IN HIS OFFICE   A238

He holds the phone and doesn't say anything.

                                                    CUT TO:

238   INT. COURTROOM - EARLY MORNING   238

The court is searched carefully by a phalanx of OFFICERS.
Metal Detectors are checked. Bomb sniffing German Shepherds
are led through the space.

239   INT. HOTEL SUITE - MORNING   239

The agents are unkempt and everyone is tired. Ruiz moves
through a cluttered room in a bathrobe with a cup of coffee.
An agent shows him a morning paper --

                         AGENT
                 Big day.
                     (shows picture in paper)
                 You're a star.

Ruiz walks over and sits across from Gordon, switching off
the radio show he's listening to. Gordon looks up from his
paper.

                         GORDON
                 Go shower. You smell.

There is a KNOCK on the front door. An AGENT goes to answer --

                                                    (CONTINUED)

                          AGENT
                Who is it?

                          SOMEBODY (V.O.)
                     (through the door)
                The Mafia. I've got his breakfast.

The agent opens the door and is handed a breakfast tray. He
puts the food in front of Ruiz who uncovers the sausage and
eggs.

An agent walking by tries to take a bite of sausage. Ruiz
stabs it with a fork --

                          RUIZ
                Fuck off.

Gordon watches the interchange --

                          GORDON
                Where's the love gone, Eddie? You'll be
                testifying for at least ten days. What if
                we stop feeding you?

Ruiz begins to eat hungrily.

                          RUIZ
                You expect me to be grateful for spending
                the rest of my life looking over my
                shoulder.

                          GORDON
                That thought makes me feel awful.

Ruiz pushes eggs into a piece of toast.

                          RUIZ
                Can't you for a second imagine none of
                this had happened? That my drugs had gone
                through. What would have been the harm? A
                few people get high who are getting high
                anyway. Your partner is still alive. We
                avoid having breakfast together. Don't
                you see this means nothing? That your
                whole life is pointless?

                          GORDON
                You're breaking my heart.

                          RUIZ
                The worst thing about you, Monty, is you
                realize the futility of what you're doing
                and you do it anyway.
                     (MORE)

                                                 (CONTINUED)

  239

                          RUIZ (cont'd)
          I wish you could see how transparent you
          are.
                (disgusted)
          This food tastes like shit.

                          GORDON
          So go shower already.

                          RUIZ
          You only got to me because you were
          tipped off by the Juarez Cartel, who's
          trying to break into Tijuana. You're
          helping them.
                (beat)
          You work for a drug dealer too, Monty.

Ruiz stands and heads for the bathroom.

                          GORDON
                (yelling after him)
          And shave. You better look nice and
          believable for the jury.

Ruiz disappears into the bathroom and slams the door behind
him.

                          GORDON (cont'd)
                (to another agent)
          It's like having another wife.

The agent laughs. There's another KNOCK on the door.

                          GORDON (cont'd)
          Who is it?

                          SOMEBODY ELSE (V.O.)
                (through the door)
          Breakfast.

Gordon and the agent look at each other.

                          SOMEBODY ELSE(V.O. Cont'd) (CONT'D)
          Hurry up. It's getting cold.

Gordon moves to the side of the door and pulls his gun. The
other agent opens the door.

A MAN with a breakfast tray enters. Gordon puts the gun to
the side of his head.

                          MAN WITH TRAY
          I'm on your side. God, you're jumpy.

239   CONTINUED: (3)   239

Gordon is momentarily confused, then goes for the bathroom
door.

                         GORDON
               Call an ambulance. Hurry.

Gordon tries the bathroom door. It's stuck. He gets it open a
crack. There's a body against the other side. He shoves.

240   INT. BATHROOM - CONTINUOUS   240

Ruiz is on the floor in convulsions.

                         GORDON
                     (yelling)
               Call the ambulance.
                     (to Ruiz)
               Don't die on me. You will not die on me.
               Do you hear me? Don't you die on me.

Ruiz's convulsions get worse, his claw-like fingers scratch
across the tile.

                                                 CUT TO:

241   OMITTED   241

242   INT. COURTROOM - SAN DIEGO - DAY   242

The court is packed. Helena and Arnie watch from the gallery.
The judge is at the bench.

The prosecutor rises --

                         PROSECUTOR
               Your honor, ladies and gentlemen of the
               jury... Because of the sudden death of
               Eduardo Ruiz, the people have decided
               that at this point we cannot continue our
               case against Carl Ayala.

The court ERUPTS. Reporters scatter. Helena cheers.

                                                 CUT TO:

243   OMITTED   243

244   INT. WHITE HOUSE OFFICE - DAY   244

Robert Wakefield enters the office of the Chief of Staff, who
looks up from what he's doing, which is reading Robert's
report, and is already mid-sentence.

                        CHIEF OF STAFF
                   Yeah, hi --
                        (waves Robert to a chair)
                   So I've got a copy of your speech here...
                        (glances down, still reading)
                   It's fantastic... So, Robert, my genuine
                   thanks. You're my choice and you're gonna
                   be great. The President is sorry he
                   hasn't been able to spend more time with
                   you. After the press conference he wants
                   to really sit down.
                        (an afterthought)
                   Oh, I got to the Post, too. Don't worry
                   about that thing with your daughter, it's
                   not news; they're willing to treat it as
                   a family matter, a personal matter.
                        (off Robert's stare)
                   Look, even if it came out, we'd turn it
                   into a qualification, *I've been in the
                   trenches of this Drug War, I have seen
                   the face of the enemy, etcetera.*

Robert just stares at him.

                                                         CUT TO:

A245   INT. JAIL CELL - DAY   A245

General Salazar sits in the same grimy cell that housed
Francisco Flores. He is sweating and his breathing is
labored. A DOCTOR enters and gives him an injection,
explaining that it will calm him down.

245   EXT. DESERT OUTSIDE TIJUANA - DAY   245

It's a reprise of the earlier desert bust... a landing strip
in the middle of nowhere, a plane landing, SUV's approaching.

This time Javi is at the wheel of one of them. News crews are
trailing behind him.

246   EXT. DESERT AIRSTRIP - LATER   246

Javi and Special Agent Hughes stand next to a giant mound of
seized cocaine, the same cocaine, in fact, Javi held briefly
at the beginning. The same teenagers from the pickup truck
have been arrested. The news crews get everything.

                        JAVIER
                   (to the press)
                   This seizure is one of the largest
                   seizures in Mexican history...
                        (MORE)

246 CONTINUED: 246

                          JAVIER (cont'd)
              It represents the first bilateral effort
              of the American DEA and the Mexican
              I.N.C.D.

A247 INT. JAIL CELL - DAY   A247

       General Salazar lies on his side, eyes and mouth open. He is
       dead. Javier looks at him through the doorway.

                          JAVIER (V.O. CONT'D)
              Today I'm very proud to announce that
              Mexico, with the help of our American
              partners, is finally winning the war
              against narcotics trafficking.

       The PRESS begins shouting questions --

                                                     CUT TO:

247 OMITTED   247

248 INT. HEADQUARTERS, I.N.C.D. - MEXICO - DAY   248

       Robert and Javi walk through the headquarters, a nondescript
       government building.

       Robert extracts photographs of the bust from a manila
       envelope. The crates of cocaine are clearly marked **"911."**

                          ROBERT
              The cocaine brand, *911,* is an East Coast
              brand, a Juarez Cartel brand, and you
              must know it usually comes through into
              El Paso?

                          JAVIER
              I'm aware of that.

                          ROBERT
              So what's it doing in Tijuana?

       Javi looks Robert Wakefield squarely in the eye. He shrugs.

                          ROBERT (cont'd)
              Let me ask you a hypothetical question:
              if Salazar worked for Madrigal and the
              Juarez cartel, and he went out of power,
              would it mean the Juarez Cartel is losing
              influence?

                          JAVIER
              It could mean that, yes.

                                                     (CONTINUED)

248   CONTINUED: 248

                              ROBERT
                    That would probably mean the Tijuana
                    Cartel is gaining power?

                              JAVIER
                    It's possible.

                              ROBERT
                    Is it possible to have a Drug Czar in
                    Mexico who isn't connected in some way to
                    one of the cartels?

          Javi thinks along time before answering.

                              JAVIER
                    Yeah, it's possible... if you're prepared
                    to die.

                                                   CUT TO:

249   EXT. AYALA FRONT YARD - AFTERNOON   249

          An outdoor party is going on. Children and adults arrive and
          mingle. Caterers work the barbecue grill. Waiters serve food
          and drink on the rolling lawn.

          Helena circles through the crowd greeting friends. She looks
          past her tree line and up the street where a telephone repair
          van is parked. She turns back toward her guests. Somebody has
          raised a cup and everyone is CHEERING.

          Helena drinks with her guests, then walks inside her house.

          AT THE FRONT GATE

          Montel Gordon walks through the gate and up the drive. He
          grabs a drink off the tray of a passing waiter. He appears
          drunk.

          Montel follows Helena into the house.

250   INT. CARL'S PRIVATE STUDY - AFTERNOON   250

          Carl hears the CHEERING outside and the sound of LAUGHTER. He
          makes a cellular telephone call.

251   INT. ARNIE METZGER'S OFFICE - AFTERNOON   251

          Arnie is in his office and answers the cell phone --

                              CARLOS (V.O.)
                    It's Saturday, Arnie. You work too hard.

                                                   (CONTINUED)

                              ARNIE
                    Carl, I'm running late. I'm coming right
                    now --

Behind Arnie in the office there is a movement of SHADOW.

251   INT. CARL'S PRIVATE STUDY - AFTERNOON   252

Carl stands at the window looking at his guests while he
talks on the phone --

                              CARLOS
                    Don't bother.

                              ARNIE (V.O.)
                    What?

                              CARLOS
                    So Arnie, when were you going to tell me
                    about the 3 million dollars we got in
                    from San Francisco two days after I got
                    arrested?

                              ARNIE (V.O.)
                    I was just waiting for the right time.

                              CARLOS
                    And you didn't feel like you could trust
                    my wife with this news?

                              ARNIE (V.O.)
                    I just didn't want to take a chance. I
                    didn't want to risk it. It could have
                    been frozen along with everything else.

                              CARLOS
                    You had it all figured out. You move into
                    my house. You raise my kids. You sleep
                    with my wife. It was a good plan, Arnie.

                              ARNIE (V.O.)
                    Carl, that's insane.

                              CARLOS
                    So my wife is lying?

                              ARNIE (V.O.)
                    Carl, think about it, if I was trying to
                    rip you off, I would have left town after
                    Ruiz was killed. I wouldn't sit next to
                    you in court listening to the dismissal.

On the front lawn CHILDREN are lined up for the ice-cream
sundae bar that is being tended by a WAITER.

>   CARLOS
>   Arnie, do think there's a difference
>   between a reason and an excuse, because I
>   don't think there is.

>   ARNIE (V.O.)
>   Carl --

>   CARLOS
>   Goodbye, Arnie.

253   INT. ARNIE METZGER'S OFFICE - AFTERNOON   253

Arnie turns around and there are TWO MEN in his office.

254   INT. CARL'S PRIVATE STUDY - AFTERNOON   254

Carl hears MUFFLED GUNSHOTS over the phone. He hangs up and
turns from the window. Helena is standing there.

>   HELENA
>   Who was that?

>   CARLOS
>   Arnie. He's not going to be able to make
>   the barbecue.

Carl and Helena share an embrace and a kiss.

>   HELENA
>   Come downstairs. Everyone is waiting.

Carl and Helena turn to leave the room and Montel Gordon is
standing in the doorway with his glass of champagne.

>   GORDON
>   Hello, Helena. What a great party.

>   CARLOS
>   Who are you?

>   GORDON
>   Nobody. I'm a nobody who arrested you,
>   but your wife is a murderer.

Gordon takes a sip of his drink. Two SECURITY OFFICERS appear
in the doorway behind him.

>   SECURITY OFFICER
>   Hey, you can't be in here.

254   CONTINUED: 254

                                  GORDON
                    I'm a cop.

                        SECURITY OFFICER
                    I don't care.

                        HELENA
                    (to the guards)
                  Throw him out of here.

The security officers grab Gordon. There is a scuffle. Gordon
falls to the floor by the window. They are wrestling. As they
wrestle, Gordon reaches out and, unnoticed, affixes a TINY
LISTENING DEVICE underneath the desk.

He continues to struggle with the guards. Helena and Carlos
start from the room.

                        GORDON
                    (calling out)
                  You didn't win, Helena. You lost
                  everything. Tell your children a nice
                  bedtime story... How you killed my
                  partner.

255   EXT. AYALA FRONT YARD - AFTERNOON   255

The guests watch as the guards eject Gordon from the
premises.

Near the gate David has stopped playing to watch the action.

Then he goes back to playing with his toy: a Spastic Jack
figure.

                                               CUT TO:

256   EXT. VERDANT NEIGHBORHOOD - MEXICO CITY - DAY   256

Javi and his convoy of armored SUV's pull up in front of the
beautiful house where earlier he deposited Rosario, Salazar's
former mistress.

Javier opens the front door and Rosario greets him by
throwing her arms around his neck. They disappear inside.

                                                 CUT TO:

257   INT. WHITE HOUSE PRESS ROOM - DAY   257

The PRESS SECRETARY stands at the familiar podium addressing
the White House Press Corps.

                                          (CONTINUED)

Robert Wakefield stands to one side with the Chief of Staff,
his lawyers, Sheridan and General Landry.

> PRESS SECRETARY
> ... a sterling reputation and close
> friend of the President, recently
> confirmed into The Office of National
> Drug Control Policy... our new Drug Czar,
> Robert Hudson Wakefield.

Applause from the assembled PRESS. The Press Secretary
signals and Robert walks to the podium. He looks back to the
Chief of Staff; he stares out at the expectant faces and
television lights and camera flashes.

> ROBERT
> (reading his prepared speech)
> The War on Drugs is a war on our nation's
> most precious resource... our children.
> Sixty-eight million children have been
> targeted by those who perpetrate this war
> and protecting those children must be
> priority number one.
> (beat)
> There has been progress and there have
> been failures, but where we have fallen
> short I see not a problem but an
> opportunity.

Robert is becoming increasingly uneasy. He glances at the
Chief of Staff who bores into him. He looks again at his
speech. With great effort he continues.

> ROBERT (cont'd)
> An opportunity to correct the mistakes of
> the past while laying a solid foundation
> for the future.
> (a long, uncomfortable beat)
> This takes not only new ideas, but
> perseverance. This takes not only
> resources, but courage. This takes not
> only government, but families.

Robert stops again as though the words are choking him.

> ROBERT (cont'd)
> I've... I've outlined a ten-point plan,
> representing a new bilateral effort...

He can't finish. Everyone stares at Robert. The crowd of
reporters senses something is wrong.

(CONTINUED)

257 CONTINUED: (2)   257

                         ROBERT (cont'd)
              I can't do this.
                   (beat)
              If there is a War on Drugs then our own
              families have become the enemy. How can
              you wage war on your own family?

He walks out of the room. The crowd waits, expecting him to
return.

Robert walks down a corridor and out of the White House.

258 EXT. WHITE HOUSE - DAY   258

A beautiful spring morning. He walks down to Pennsylvania
Avenue. He hails a cab and gets in. The cab pulls away.

259 INT. CHURCH BASEMENT - DAY   259

A twelve step meeting is in progress. Caroline shares from
her seat.

                         CAROLINE
              On the good days I feel like I get it,
              like it all makes sense. I can stay in
              the moment. I don't have to control
              everything in the future. And I believe
              everything is going to work out fine.
                   (beat)
              On the bad days, I just want to grab the
              phone and start dialing numbers. I want
              to pull my hair and run through the
              streets screaming.
                   (beat)
              But, thanks to the people I've met in
              these rooms, people like Margaret and Jim
              and Sarah, people who've taught me how to
              listen, I'm pretty sure I'll make it
              through today.

Caroline is finished sharing.

                         VOICE (O.S.)
              Would you like to share?

We pan over to reveal Robert and Barbara sitting next to
Caroline.

                                              (CONTINUED)

259   CONTINUED: 259

> ROBERT
> My name is Robert. This is my wife,
> Barbara. We're Caroline's parents. We're
> just hear to listen.

                                               CUT TO:

260   OMIT.   260

261   EXT. AYALA HOME - NIGHT   261

The house is dark and silent. The van is parked up the
street.

262   INT. VAN - NIGHT   262

Gordon listens through a headset, his expression set.

> CARLOS (V.O.)
> (over a listening device)
> We're back up and running. Completely
> untouchable. Completely.

                                               CUT TO:

263   EXT. BASEBALL FIELD - TIJUANA - NIGHT   263

A bank of lights CRANKS on. Then ANOTHER and ANOTHER.

In a wider shot we see an illuminated baseball field where a
children's pickup game is in progress.

In the crowd, Javi serenely watches the game.

                          THE END

STILLS

MICHAEL DOUGLAS
as Robert Wakefield

CATHERINE ZETA-JONES
as Helena Ayala

BENICIO DEL TORO
as Javier Rodriguez

DON CHEADLE
as Montel Gordon

LUIS GUZMAN
as Ray Castro

DENNIS QUAID
as Arnie Metzger

ERIKA CHRISTENSEN
as Caroline Wakefield

ALBERT FINNEY
as Chief of Staff

BENJAMIN BRATT
as Juan Obregon

JAMES BROLIN
as General Ralph Landry

Top: Scene 79: Caroline Wakefield spends the night in a juvenile detention center.
Bottom: Scene A57: Javier Rodriguez and Manolo Sanchez wait to meet General Salazar.

Top: Scene 140: Robert Wakefield discovers Caroline using drugs.
Bottom: Scene 129: Arnie Metzger and Helena Ayala discuss Carl's situation.

Top: Scene D115: Javier warns Manolo not to screw up.
Bottom: Scene 75: Francisco Flores *(Clifton Collins)* is tortured by General Salazar's guard.

Top: Scene 103: General Salazar *(Thomas Millian)* interrogates Francisco Flores.
Bottom: Scene 115: Caroline and Seth *(Topher Grace)* go to buy drugs.

Top: Scene 88: Robert and Barbara Wakefield *(Amy Irving)* worry about their missing daughter.
Bottom: Scene 218: Helena going to be strip searched at the border.

Top: Scene C154: Robert meets with General Salazar to discuss the war on drugs.
Bottom: Scene 177: Ray Castro and Montel Gordon escort Eduardo Ruiz *(Miguel Ferrer)* into the courthouse for his testimony.

Top: Scene 210: Javier gives the DEA information on General Salazar.
Bottom: Scene 199: Helena shows Juan Obregon the newest way to transport cocaine.

Scene 259: Robert and Barbara listen to Caroline's speech at rehab.

Steven Soderbergh, director/cinematographer, lines up a shot.

Top: Night exterior shooting scene A115 in Nogales, Mexico which doubles for Tijuana.
Bottom: Stephen Gaghan and Steven Soderbergh on location in Washington, D.C.

166

Top: Stephen Gaghan and Tim Golden *(Story Consultant)* dressed as extras for the Georgetown cocktail party.
Bottom: Behind the scenes at the San Ysidro border crossing at San Diego-Tijuana.

CAST AND CREW CREDITS

USA FILMS Presents
In Association With INITIAL ENTERTAINMENT GROUP
A BEDFORD FALLS/LAURA BICKFORD Production

| DON CHEADLE | BENICIO DEL TORO | MICHAEL DOUGLAS |
| LUIS GUZMAN | DENNIS QUAID | CATHERINE ZETA-JONES |

TRAFFIC

Casting by
DEBRA ZANE, C.S.A.

Music by
CLIFF MARTINEZ

Costume Design by
LOUISE FROGLEY

Edited by
STEPHEN MIRRIONE

Production Design by
PHILIP MESSINA

Executive Producers
RICHARD SOLOMON
MIKE NEWELL
CAMERON JONES
GRAHAM KING
ANDREAS KLEIN

Produced by
EDWARD ZWICK
MARSHALL HERSKOVITZ
LAURA BICKFORD

Screenplay by
STEPHEN GAGHAN

Directed by
STEVEN SODERBERGH

Unit Production Manager
FREDERICK W. BROST

First Assistant Director
GREGORY JACOBS

Second Assistant Director
TREY BATCHELOR

CAST

(In Order of Appearance)

Javier Rodríguez	Benicio Del Toro
Manolo Sanchez	Jacob Vargas
Desert Truck Drivers	Andrew Chavez
	Michael Saucedo
General Arturo Salazar	Tomas Milian
Salazar Soldier/The Torturer	Jose Yenque
Salazar Soldier #2	Emilio Rivera
Lawyer Rodman	Michael O'Neill
Robert Wakefield	Michael Douglas
Clerk	Russell G. Jones
State Capitol Reporter #1	Lorene Hetherington
State Capitol Reporter #2	Eric Collins
DEA Agents (CalTrans)	Beau Holden
	Peter Stader
	James Lew
	Jeremy Fitzgerald
	Russell Solberg
Ray Castro	Luis Guzman
Montel Gordon	Don Cheadle
DEA Agents (Trailer)	Don Snell
	Enrique Murciano
	Gary Carlos Cervantes
Ruiz's Secretary	Leticia Bombardier
Eduardo Ruiz	Miguel Ferrer
Ruiz's Assistant	Carl Ciarfalio
Van Driver	Steve Lambert
Van Passenger	Gilbert Rosales

Dea Agents (Public Storage)	Rick Avery
	Mario Roberts
	Eileen Weisinger
	Keii Johnston
	Mike Watson
	Kurt Lott
	Lincoln Simonds
	Steve Tomaski
	Buck McDancer
	John Callery
	Ousaun Elam
	Brian Avery
F*****-up Bowman	Corey Spears
Vanessa	Majandra Delfino
Seth Abrahms	Topher Grace
Caroline Wakefield	Erika Christensen
David Ayala	Alec Roberts
Helena Ayala	Catherine Zeta-Jones
Helena's Friends	Rena Sofer
	Stacey Travis
	Jennifer Barker
Parking Valet	Dean Faulkner
Chief of Staff	Albert Finney
Jeff Sheridan	D.W. Moffett
General Ralph Landry	James Brolin
Tourist Woman	Daniella Kuhn
Tourist Man	Brandon Keener
Himself	Governor Bill Weld
Partygoer #1	George Blumenthal
Lobbyist	Stephen Dunham

Himself . . . . Senator Don Nickles
Economist . . . . Margaret Travolta
Himself. . . . . Senator Harry Reid
Himself . . . . Jeff Podolsky
Partygoer #2. . . . . Jewelle Bickford
Herself. . . . . Senator Barbara Boxer
Himself . . . . Senator Orrin Hatch
Himself . . . . Senator Charles Grassley
Partygoer #3 . . . . Dave Hager
Partygoer #4 . . . . Tucker Smallwood
Carlos Ayala . . . . Steven Bauer
Ana Sanchez . . . . Marisol Padilla Sanchez
Barbara Wakefield. . . . . Amy Irving
Arnie Metzger . . . . Dennis Quaid
Francisco Flores . . . . Clifton Collins, Jr.
Salazar Soldiers. . . . . Victor Quintero
Toby Holguin
Ramiro Gonzalez
Social Worker. . . . . Viola Davis
Prosecutor Ben Williams . . . . James Pickens, Jr.
Attorney Michael Adler . . . . Peter Riegert
Judge Reed . . . . Elaine Kagan
ADA Dan Collier . . . . John Slattery
Arrested Man in Apartment. . . . . Jim Ortega
Tackled Man #1. . . . . Greg Boniface
Tackled Man #2. . . . . Tom Rosales
Customs Official . . . . Rudy M. Camacho
Dealer . . . . Vonte Sweet
Hotel Deskman . . . . Ed Breving
Tigrillo/Obregón Assassin . . . . Yul Vazquez
Agent Hughes . . . . Jack Conley
Agent Johnson . . . . Eddie Velez
Director of EPIC . . . . Craig N. Chretien
Assistant Director of EPIC. . . . . John Brown
DEA Representative . . . . Mike Siegel
Porfilio Madrigal. . . . . Joel Torres
Marty . . . . Steve Rose
Rehab Counselor . . . . Kimber Fritz
Witness #1 . . . . Harsh Nayyar
Witness #2. . . . . Mary Pat Gleason
Man on Street . . . . Vincent Ward
Juan Obregón . . . . Benjamin Bratt
Pablo Obregón . . . . Jsu Garcia
Polygraph Administrator . . . . Gregory Estevane
Polygraph Assistant . . . . Alex Procopio
Mrs. Castro . . . . Rita Gomez
Teacher . . . . Kaizaad Navroze Kotwal
"John". . . . . David Jensen
Waiter #1. . . . . Jay Fernando Krymis
Waiter #2 . . . . Mike Malone
Doctor . . . . Rene Pereyra
Press Secretary . . . . Kymberly S. Newberry
Ayala Security #1 . . . . Carroll Schumacher
Ayala Security #2. . . . . Ben Scott
Meeting Leader . . . . Michael Showers

THE FILMMAKERS

Stunt Coordinator . . . . John Robotham
Consultant. . . . . Tim Golden
Art Director . . . . Keith P. Cunningham
Set Decorator. . . . . . . Kristen Toscano Messina, S.D.S.A.
Camera Operator . . . . Gary Jay
A Camera First Assistant. . . . . Barry Idoine
B Camera First Assistant . . . . Duane C. Manwiller
Production Sound Mixer . . . . Paul Ledford, C.A.S.
Boom Operators   Keenan Wyatt
                                        Joseph F. Brennan
Production Supervisor . . . . Robin L. Le Chanu
Production Accountant. . . . . Sonny Ritscher
Script Supervisor . . . . Annie Welles
Technical Consultant . . . . Craig N. Chretien
Assistant Art Directors. . . . . Blair Huizingh
                                    Valerie Nadja Lancelot
Set Designers   Greg Berry
                                        Maya Shimoguchi
                                      Barbara Ann Spencer
Property Master . . . . Steven B. Melton
Assistant Property Masters . . . . Lance Larson
                                          Melody Miller
Art Department Coordinator . . . . . . Wylie Young Griffin
Art Department Assistant . . . . Eric Bryant
Assistant Set Decorator . . . . Shana Sigmond
Leadman . . . . Jason Bedig
Set Dressers   Dale E. Anderson
                                          Brent Blom
                                          Gary Brewer
                                          Alan Easley
                                        Brooke Sartorius
On-Set Dresser . . . . Mike Malone
A Camera Second Assistant . . . . James Apted
B Camera Second Assistant. . . . . Glenn Brown
Camera Loader . . . . Stacy de la Motte
Still Photographer. . . . . Bob Marshak
Camera Production Assistant. . . . . Caz Duffy
Projectionist . . . . E. J. Butch Ertel
Additional Boom Operator. . . . . Earl Sampson
Utility Sound . . . . Richard Kite
Chief Lighting Technician . . . . James Plannette
Best Boy Electric . . . . Eric Wycoff
Electrician . . . . Russell Ayer
Rigging Gaffer . . . . R. Michael De Chellis
Rigging Best Boy Electric . . . . Eric Wolfson-Sagot
Key Grip . . . . Herb Ault
Best Boy Grip . . . . Kevin "Rambo" Fitzgerald
Camera Grip. . . . . Paul Threlkeld
Grip . . . . Kyle Carden
Rigging Key Grip . . . . Andreas Crawford
Rigging Best Boy Grip. . . . . Dustin Ault
Grip Production Assistant . . . . Kelvin Hunter
Second 2nd Assistant Director . . . . . Basti van der Woude

Set Production Assistants . . . . Keri Bruno
Michael La Corte
Lynn Struiksma
DGA Trainee . . . . Beryl Cohen
First Assistant Avid Editor . . . . Douglas Crise
First Assistant Film Editor . . . . Keith Sauter
Second Assistant Editor . . . . Norman Walker
Editorial Production Assistant . . . . Denise Marquez
Special Effects Coordinator . . . . Kevin Hannigan
Special Effects Foreman . . . . Werner Hahnlein
Special Effects Set Foreman . . . . Anthony Simonaitis
Special Effects Technicians. . . . . Michael D. Roundy
William D. Harrison
Costume Supervisor . . . . Joyce Kogut
Key Costumer . . . . Garet Reilly
Costumer . . . . Lizz Wolf
Set Costumer for Mr. Douglas . . . . Fran Allgood
Set Costumers . . . . Edward T. Hanley
Annie Miller
Shoshana Rubin
Richard Schoen
Tailor . . . . Francisco Mares
Cutter/Fitter . . . . Elizabeth Besio
Makeup Department Head . . . . Kathrine James
Key Makeup Artist . . . . Loretta James Demasi
Hair Department Heads . . . . Bonnie Clevering
Kathrine Gordon
Hair Stylist . . . . Roxanne Wightman
Location Manager . . . . Ken Lavet
Additional Location Manager . . . . George Herthel
Assistant Location Managers . . . . Quentin Halliday
P. Caleb Duffy
Location Production Assistant . . . . Anthony Rico
First Assistant Accountant . . . . Sonya Lunsford
Second Assistant Accountants . . . . Lisa Carey
Jeffrey C. Harris
Jason Hinkel
Payroll Accountant. . . . . Renee D. Czarapata
Construction Accountant . . . . Marisol Jimenez
Accounting Clerk . . . . Alice Prochazkova
Production Coordinator . . . . Karen Jarnecke
Assistant Production Coordinators . . . . . . Angie Lee Cobbs
Clelio Boccato
Production Office Assistants . . . . Carrie Brody
Will Sandoval
Studio Teacher . . . . Thomas J. McGowan
Translators . . . . Rene Pereyra
Luis M. Rodríquez Villa
Mr. Del Toro's Dialect Coach . . . . Alan Shaterian
Casting Associate . . . . Terri R. Taylor
Casting Assistant . . . . Pamela Lynn Thomas
Extras Casting. . . . . Rich King Casting
Publicist. . . . . Spooky Stevens
Assistant to Mr. Soderbergh . . . . Caitlin Maloney
Assistant to Ms. Bickford . . . . Valentina Aulisi

Assistant to Mr. Zwick . . . . Graham Larsen
Assistant to Mr. Herskovitz . . . . Josh Gummersall
Assistant to Mr. Solomon . . . . Robin Cohen
Assistant to Mr. Newell & Mr. Jones . . . William Butler-Sloss
Assistant to Mr. King. . . . . Andrea Tagliareni
Assistant to Mr. Douglas . . . . Robert Mitas
Assistant to Ms. Zeta-Jones . . . . Julianne Berkowitz
Cast Assistants . . . . Brumby Broussard
Mark Dometrovich
John Falvey
Jason Rider
Construction Coordinator . . . . Chris Snyder
General Foreman . . . . William Gideon
Paint Supervisor. . . . . Hank Giardina
Office Foreman/Purchaser . . . . John Moore
Location Foreman . . . . Gerard Forrest
Propmaker Foremen . . . . John B. Bullard
James Paniagua
Dale Snyder
Plaster Foreman . . . . Adam L. Barker
Labor Foremen . . . . Robert Fidalgo
Louie Esparza, Jr.
Anthony J. Saenz, Jr.
Welder/Ironman. . . . . Bud Kucia
Propmaker Gangbosses . . . . Jeffrey Brooks
Jerrold F. Brooks
Bill Duffin
Michael Jon Duffin
Alfred J. Ransdell
Curtis A. Yackel
Propmaker . . . . Christopher Forrest
Paint Foremen . . . . Steven Kerlagun
Clyde Zimmerman
Signwriter. . . . . Jerry Miller
Painters . . . . Jay E. Brooks
Joseph A. Northrop
Chad Simpson
Greensmen   Richard Boris
Andrew Nowling
Transportation Coordinator . . . . Jon Carpenter
Transportation Captain. . . . . Shane Greedy
Transportation Co-Captain. . . . . Richard Bennetti
Transportation Dispatcher . . . . Doreen L. Carpenter
Film Runner. . . . . John Quittner
Drivers . . . .
James C. Alfonso   Chris Beanes
Loren Bess   Frank Alan Butler
Gary Cheek   Robert Chookhachian
Charles Conn   Gary D. Cruise
Dale A. Douglas   Robert W. Dulys
Guy A. Duquette   Bernard A. Glavin
Leon L. Glavin   Chris Gorden
Billy Grace   Phillip Helman
Mike Hutmacher   Jonny R. Johnson
J.T. Lannen   James V. Lingle

Drivers (*Continued*) . . . .
  Tony Mercier   Ken Merritt
  Tom Neal   Robert L. Neilson
  Dominic Jack Pizzo, Sr.   Curtis Randoll
  Chance Robertson   George Chip Robinson
  Sean C. Ryan   William Mark Spencer
  Paul Tumber   Gordon R. Winkle
Set Medic . . . . Keri Littledeer
Technical Advisor . . . . Chic Daniel
                Reel Deal Technical Advisors
Set Security Coordinator. . . . . John Ramirez
Catering . . . . Gourmet On Location
Chef. Antoine Mascaro
Catering Assistants. . . . . Carlos Flores
                 Manuel D. Cocar
               Guillermo Villegas
Craft Service . . . . Ronald E. Hairston
                Tamiko Hairston
              Ronald Hairston, Jr.

Supervising Sound Editor
Re-Recording Mixer
Larry Blake

Post-Production Supervisor . . . . Caitlin Maloney
Post-Production Assistants. . . . . P. Caleb Duffy
              Meaghan F. McLaughlin
Dialogue Editor . . . . Aaron Glascock
Assistant Sound Editor. . . . . F. Scott Taylor
Post-Production Sound Services . . . Weddington Productions
Weddington Transfer . . . . Mark Coffey
                 Rusty Amodeo
Foley by . . . . Alicia Irwin
                 Dawn Fintor
Foley Mixer . . . . David Betancourt
Foley Recorded at . . . . Twentieth Century Fox
Foley Editors. . . . . Rick Mitchell
                 John Murray
Re-Recorded at . . . . Swelltone Labs/New Orleans
Mix Assistants   Matt Coby
                 Jay Gallagher

Musicians

Music Programming and Orchestrations . . . . . . Jeff Rona
Textural Constructions, Guitar . . . SPLaTTeRCeLL (d. torn)
Guitar . . . . Michael Brook
Master of the 4-String Electric Bassius O' Pheilius . . . . Flea
     Flea appears courtesy of Warner Bros. Records
Electric Piano . . . . Herbie Hancock
Percussion. . . . . Alex Acuna
                 Paulinho Da Costa
Electric Piano. . . . . Mark Pelsone
Music Mixed by. . . . . Alan Meyerson
Assistant Engineers. . . . . Gregg Silk
                 Kevin Globerman

Synth Recording . . . . Tobias Enhus
Contractor. . . . . David Low
Score Mixed at . . . . Media Ventures
Music Consultant . . . . Frankie Pine
Mexico Sequences Digital Visual Effects . . . . . Cinesite, Inc.
Production . . . . Mike Sullo
                 Carole Cowley
                 Rick Benoit
Senior Colorist. . . . . Julius Friede
Junior Colorist . . . . Jill Bogdanowicz
Digital Compositors   Steven Wright
                 Kama Moiha
                 Serena Naramore
Editorial. . . . . Shawn J. Broes
                 Paul Howarth
Technical Assistants . . . . Brian Shows
                 Todd Sarsfield
                 Tony Sgueglia
Digital Asset Manager . . . . Vincent Lavares
Digital Imaging Coordinator. . . . . Erik Hakanen
Digital Imaging Operator . . . . Kristopher Gregg
Titles & Opticals . . . . Howard Anderson Company
Negative Cutter . . . . Gary Burritt
Color Timer. . . . . Dana Ross
Ektachrome Reversal Process . . . . Les Meek/Frank Holmes
                 Laboratories, Inc.
Dailies Telecine/Track Negative . . . NT Audio Video Film Labs
Cutting Continuity . . . . Masterwords
Camera Dollies by . . . . Chapman/Leonard
                 Studio Equipment, Inc.
Production Legal. . . . . Robert Darwell
               Troop Steuber Pasich
                 Reddick & Tobey
Clearance Services . . . . Jay Floyd/Now Clear This!
Insurance . . . . Great Northern Brokerage

San Diego Crew

Assistant Production Coordinator . . . . Carrie Black
Production Office Assistants . . . . Betsy Dennis
                 Amy Sterner
Set Dresser . . . . Manuel Castillo
Grip. Carlos Boiles

Mexico Crew

Production Manager . . . . Anna Roth
Assistant Director. . . . . Adrian Grunberg Kaufman
Assistant Cameraman . . . . Joachin Cervera Buenfil
Location Manager . . . . Daniel Martinez
Location Assistant. . . . . Antonio Mata Sanchez
Assistant Production Coordinator . . . . . . Sylvia Remington
Production Office Assistant . . . . . . Meaghan F. McLaughlin

El Paso Crew

Location Assistant . . . . R. Michael Charske
Assistant Production Coordinator . . . . Lilli Heinrich
Production Office Assistant . . . . Diana C. Tulk
Driver . . . . Dusty Tulk

Cincinnati Crew

Production Manager. . . . . Patricia S. Chapman
Location Manager . . . . Deirdre Costa
Assistant Production Coordinator. . . . . Molly A. Donnellon
Production Office Assistants . . . . Sara Brenna Hine
Keith Heileman
Laborer . . . . Adam Snyder

Washington, D.C. Crew

Location Manager . . . . Peggy Pridemore
Location Casting by . . . . Kimberly Skyrme

"Give The Po' Man a Break"
Written by Norman Cook
Performed by Fatboy Slim
Courtesy of Astralwerks Records

"On the Rhodes Again"
Written by Skye Edwards, Paul Godfrey and Ross Godfrey
Performed by Morcheeba
Courtesy of Sire Records Group/Warner Music U.K. Ltd
By Arrangement with Warner Special Products

"Piano Sonata No. 1 In F Minor"
Written by Ludwig van Beethoven
Performed by Wilhelm Kempff
Courtesy of Universal International Music, BV
Under License from Universal Music Enterprise.

"Going Under (Love & Insanity Dub) - K&D Sessions"
Written by Glyn Bush, Richard Whittingham and Patrick Plummer
Performed by Rockers Hi-Fi
Courtesy of Warner Bros. Records Inc./Warner Music Germany
By Arrangement with Warner Special Products

"An Ending (Ascent)"
Written and Performed by Brian Eno
Courtesy of Astralwerks Records

Soundtrack Available on TVT Soundtrax

"Child With a Hoop" Courtesy of
The Estate of Rafael Coronel

Scene from "Dynasty" with music, "Rough Days" by Peter Myers,
Courtesy of Paramount Pictures

"Blind Date" ©2000 Universal Television Enterprises, Inc. All
Rights Reserved.Courtesy of Universal Studios Licensing, Inc.

Special Thanks

U. S. Customs
Drug Enforcement Administration
El Paso Intelligence Center
U.S. General Services Administration
U.S. District Court for the Southern District
of Ohio, Eastern Division
Joseph P. Kinneary Federal Courthouse
Columbus, Ohio

El Paso Film Commission
Greater Cincinnati and Northern Kentucky Film Commission
Las Cruces Film Office
Ohio Film Commission
San Diego Film Commission
Tucson Film Office
Film Commission, Sonora, Mexico
Warner Bros. "The West Wing" Set

Illa Brown
Karyn Cody
Juan Coronel
Lisa Fairchild
Raymond Kelly
Charles Labella
Dennis Murphy
Terry Parham
Catherine H. Shaw

Copyright © 2000 Compulsion, Inc.
All Rights Reserved